I0549520

The Allure of

High Places

a novel

Zoe Murdock

H.O.T. Press

Publishing fine books since 1983

Published by
H.O.T. Press
Ojai, California 93023
www.hotpresspublishing.com

Copyright 2025 by Zoe Murdock
All rights reserved.

ISBN: 0-923178-45-7
ISBN - 13: 978-0-923178-45-1

For Doc,

without whom this book would not exist,
without whom I would not exist.

Acknowledgments

I am deeply indebted to the members of the Ojai Writing Workshop who gave me invaluable feedback and insight as I worked through the many drafts of this novel.

The Allure of
High Places

Chapter 1

Maddie's so mad. She's nearly eight, but Momma still won't let her go down to the condo playground. No. She'll be stuck up here on the seventh-floor balcony forever watching the other kids play. If she was down there, she wouldn't be riding the merry-go-round or slippin' down the slide with the little kids. She'd be flying high on the swings with the older boys. She knows how to do it, so why can't she?

She knows why. It's because Momma's an old scaredy-cat who won't go out of the condo for anything, and she won't let Maddie go out either. She says, "The city's no place for a girl, Maddie. It's not safe. Thieves on every corner waiting for you to make one lousy mistake. Don't you go down there, Maddie. You hear me?"

"Yes, Momma." She's heard it so many times, she can hear it even when she's not saying it.

Daddy's not like that. He'd let her go out into the world, if it didn't upset Momma so much. He tries to make up for it by bringing her books and telling her stories when he comes home from one of his long trips to Japan. She loves the stories and the books about the culture of the people and the clothes they wear. The temples and shrines. The cherry trees. She's got books on Japanese art and history. A book about the wise teacher, Buddha. She especially loves her books on Asian birds: the White-bellied Woodpecker. The Black-capped Kingfisher with that beautiful flash of bright blue on his wings. She loves birds.

She doesn't want to be a scaredy-cat like Momma. She wants to go down into the city, get in a taxi, and ride to the giant blue-windowed skyscraper where Daddy works. She'd take the escalator to the very top floor, sit in Daddy's big chair, and look out over the tall buildings to where the clouds billow high above the far away mountains. She'd stay there all day watching the sun move across the sky. Daddy's told her how beautiful it is, but she needs to see it for herself.

What she really needs to see is Japan. Last time Daddy came home, he told her about Enoshima Island, a place where wild cats ride the escalators all night while the people sleep. He said he rode to the top of the island with the cats and saw the white peacock spread its shimmering feathers under a full moon. "I wish you'd been with me, Maddie. It was glorious."

She said, "I wish I'd been there too, Daddy. Will you take me sometime?"

He gave her a sad smile and told her about the whispering Buddha that lives in the dark tunnels beneath the island. He didn't know what the Buddha whispered, but it must have been important. After all, the Buddha is a wise teacher who helps people find silence in their minds, so they can be peaceful and calm. She wishes the Buddha would help her stop the screaming silence that she hears sometimes.

There's no use thinking about Japan. Momma will never let her go there or anywhere else. She'll be stuck up on the balcony forever watching the boys swing. Why don't they jump off the swing and see if they can fly? That's what she'd do, if she was down there.

She wonders if the boys ever look up and see her. If they do, what do they see? A lonely girl in a white princess dress stuck behind black balcony bars? A girl who can never do anything, except watch?

She hears something inside the condo. She holds her breath to listen. No. It's not a sound, it's silence. Momma stopped singing her sad cowgirl songs. She must have finished her bath.

"Maaa... die, could you do me a favor, honey?"

"Oh no." Momma's using her sugary voice. She must want Maddie to do something she doesn't want to do.

She clamps her hands over her ears, but Momma's voice bleeds through. "Maddie, be a good girl. Bring me a fresh bottle of whiskey, would you?"

She doesn't want to be a good girl. She wants to be herself, whoever that is. How can she know who she is if she's never lived in the real world and doesn't have a single friend? If she just had one person to talk to when Daddy's on one of his trips. Someone to have fun with when Momma's in the bathtub drinking whiskey or treating her like she doesn't exist.

After one last look at the boys on the swings, she gets up and goes inside. She twirls across the smooth mahogany floor, her honey-blond hair flying out, the soft white fabric of her satin princess dress spinning around her waist. She's Odette, the ballerina swan in Swan Lake. She pirouettes for her prince and blows him a kiss, hoping his love will be strong enough to break the curse of Momma's fear.

"Damn it, Maddie! Get that whiskey up here! Now!"

She races to the kitchen, pushes a chair to the counter, climbs up, reaches into the top shelf. Nothing there. She stands on her tiptoes and reaches in deeper. There it is. One last bottle. She'd better tell Daddy. It's not good when

Momma runs out of whiskey. She does things she's sorry about later and keeps saying whiskey's the only thing that keeps her sane.

Maddie doesn't understand how the whiskey helps, but she does go crazy sometimes. She mutters and wanders around like she's looking for something she can't find.

"Maaa…die! You'll be sorry if I have to come down there."

"I'm coming, Momma! I'm almost there!"

She races up the curved white marble steps, runs down the hall, and throws open the bathroom door. She squints, trying not to see Momma's blotched skin, the yellow hair stuck to the side of her face, her troubled green eyes.

"Why do you stay in the bathtub so long, Momma. It makes you–"

"What?"

"Nothing. I just mean, you're so beautiful, and–"

"Who cares. I'm not going anywhere. Now give me that bottle."

Maddie shoves it into her hands and races back downstairs.

She wanders the living room and ends up in the corner at White Bird's gold cage. His eyes look troubled, like Momma's. Maddie knows why. He needs freedom. She's thought about setting him free, but she can't make herself do it. White Bird is Momma's birthday bird. She can't let him go, even though she's not sure Momma likes him anymore. She used to tweet at him when she'd go by his cage, and she taught him to sing the songs of other birds. She and Momma used to laugh their heads off when White Bird sang like a tweety-bird or cawed at the top of his lungs like a crow, or made the long haunting cry of a loon. Did they really have that much fun?

She presses her nose against the cold gold bars of the cage. "I know why you're sad, White Bird. You're trapped, like me. We're all trapped. Even Momma's trapped, and Daddy's trapped too. He doesn't know how to make Momma happy. He brings her presents from Japan, beautiful silk Kimonos and special black lacquer and mother-of-pearl boxes and earrings and clips. Nothing helps. I don't know why, White Bird, but she's getting worse, and I don't know what I'm supposed to do. I wish Daddy was here."

White Bird doesn't care. He won't even look at her.

"Please, White Bird. Don't ignore me. That's what Momma does."

She opens the cage door and nuzzles her finger against White Bird's cheek. She tweets and twitters and chirps, trying to get him to sing along.

He just stares at the newspaper floor.

What else can she do?

Maybe he'd feel better if he had some fresh air and could see the animal clouds galloping across the sky.

She slides his cage to the balcony window.

White Bird won't look out. He won't chirp. He won't sing. It's like he's given up doing anything. He'll die if he gives up completely.

It would break her heart if White Bird dies. She already lost little Sami, her preying mantis friend, so she knows how bad that feels.

She has to set White Bird free.

Momma will kill her.

"But he'll die, if he's not free." She can't let him die. She should set him free and tell Momma she doesn't know what happened. Say, it wasn't her fault.

Momma won't believe her. She'll send her to bed without supper and tell Daddy what a bad daughter he has.

He'll get that disappointed look on his face that Maddie can't bear. She wants Daddy to be happy when he's home, so she can be happy, and maybe Momma can be happy too.

It seems like they used to be happy. She has a far away memory of Daddy coming home from a business dinner looking handsome in his black tuxedo and starched white shirt. When he saw Momma on the couch, showing off her pretty legs, he put on some music and asked her to dance. Momma gave him a flirty smile and went upstairs to put on lipstick and a long, slinky green dress made of silk. She floated down the stairs like she was on a cloud and ended up in Daddy's arms. They danced all around the living room with the shine of love in their eyes. Then, when the music changed, they gathered her in and they all danced together.

That might have been a dream, but it seems real.

Maddie takes a closer look at White Bird. He hasn't eaten any of the sunflower seeds and dried blueberries she gave him last night. His water dish is still full. If she doesn't do something, he'll die of thirst.

If White Bird dies, he'll be gone anyway. She might as well set him free, so he can live. Or, maybe, she could just let him out of his cage for a minute. He could fly around the living room and feel like he was free. Then she could put him back in his cage and nobody would have to know.

She sticks her hand in the cage and jiggles her finger next to his feet. "Come, little White Bird. I'll let you out. But only for a minute. Okay? Then you have to go back in your cage. You promise?"

White Bird doesn't move.

She jiggles her finger again. "White Bird. Pretty Bird. Please, come out."

She feels his prickly claws on her finger and quickly lifts him out. He takes off, circling around the ceiling in a crazy way, barely missing the walls and the crystal candles in the chandelier. It's amazing how fast he can fly. How did he learn to do that when he's never been free?

He swoops down, flies past her face, and darts straight out the window. He lands on the balcony railing and looks back at her with a sparkle of mischief in his eyes. With one loud squawk, he's gone.

She runs to the railing and leans out as far as she can, looking for him in every direction. She can't see him anywhere. Oh no! How's she going to get him back in his cage before Momma finds out and, for sure, before Daddy gets home.

White Bird flies back, flapping his wings wildly and squawking at the top of his lungs, like he's screaming, "I'm free. I'm free. Come be free with me, Maddie."

She yells, "Please, White Bird. I want to fly with you, but it's time to get back in your cage."

He flies away, then comes back again and again, squawking loudly and flapping his wings in her face, as if he's impatient for her to fly with him. She's going to be in such big trouble for letting him go, she might as well do what he wants. White Bird can teach her how to fly, and they can go to Neverland where she can do whatever she wants.

She squeezes through the black iron rails, holds on, and balances on the edge of the balcony, feeling a cold rush of excitement and fear. A gust of wind hits her face, whipping her hair into her eyes, and now she can't see.

She holds her breath and releases the grip on one hand to push back her hair. White Bird swoops in over her head, screaming at the top of his lungs that she's got to come fly with him, and now, she's falling.

No, she's not falling. She's flying. She just needs to flap her wings.

A whoosh of air ruffles her princess dress up like wings. She flaps them, but they don't catch air. The ground's rushing towards her. She screams, "Help me, White Bird?"

She lands with a whoosh in a soft bed of white blossoms that crumple down to hard ground. She lies still, catching her breath, checking her arms and legs for any cuts or bruises.

There's not a bit of hurt anywhere. It's like her fairytale godmother dropped out of the sky and saved her. Or maybe it was Peter Pan, or probably, it was White Bird.

She sees Gardener racing toward her with a shocked look on his face. He stops and stares down at her with his hands on his hips. "What happened? Are you okay?"

"I'm fine."

His eyes show he doesn't believe her. "How'd you do that, Missy? How'd you fall from way up there and not get hurt?" He looks up at the balcony and back down at her.

"That's not true, Gardener. I didn't fall. I was flying. Didn't you see me?"

"Sure. Sure. I saw you." He gives her the hint of a smile and pulls her up by the hand. "We'd better get you upstairs, quick. Your Momma's probably going crazy trying to find you."

"I doubt it. She's in the bathtub."

They take the elevator to the seventh floor and Gardener rings the doorbell.

Finally, Momma opens the door wearing her black silk kimono with pink cherry blossoms and a white crane. Her wet, yellow hair is twisted up and held in place with a black mother-of-pearl clip. She gives Gardener a nervous smile, which tells Maddie she's trying to be nice but she really doesn't want him there.

Gardener steps to the side and Momma sees Maddie for the first time. Her smile flies away. "What's going on, Maddie? What'd you do?"

"I didn't do anything."

"It looks like you went outside. I told you not to go out there."

Gardener tells Momma the whole story of how Maddie went flying off the balcony and landed in the flowerbed without a scratch.

Momma looks scared. "No! No! That can't be true!" She falls to her knees and hugs Maddie so hard it hurts. She plasters little kisses all over her head that hurt even more than her hugging. "Please, Maddie," she wails, "don't go out there! Do you hear me? I can't lose another one. I can't."

"What do you mean, Momma. What did you lose?"

Momma hugs her harder and whimpers. "Promise me, Maddie. Promise."

"Okay, Momma. I promise." She says the words, but she knows they're not true. She's like *Alice in Wonderland*, she can't go back to how she was yesterday. She's a different person now. She's been flying with White Bird, and from now on she just wants to fly.

Chapter 2

Maddie sits next to Momma on the sofa looking at pretty clothes in *Glamour Magazine* when Daddy calls to say he's almost home. Momma hangs up and shoots her a mean look. "Don't you say anything about that bird, Maddie. You hear me?"

That's so frustrating. She really wanted to tell Daddy about flying, and now, she can't. It's not fair.

Momma looks suspicious. "In fact, I think you should go to bed."

"No, Momma! Please! I'm not tired, and we haven't had dinner."

"I'll bring you something later. Now, go!"

Maddie *goes*, but she goes slow, like the straw man in the *Wizard of Oz*, slipping and sliding up the white marble stairs, wobbling down the hall to her bedroom on the straw legs of a scarecrow. She closes the door and presses her forehead against the cold wood. "Why are you so mean, Momma?"

She sits on the edge of her bed and waits for the screaming sound of silence to arrive. When it does, she clamps her hands over her ears and falls back into the white satin down of her quilt. She closes her eyes, lifts her princess dress, and wills herself to disappear as it floats down.

It doesn't work. She's too worried about what Momma's going to tell Daddy about White Bird. Will he shake his head in disappointment? What if he gets mad? No, Daddy never gets mad at her. That's only Momma.

She grips the gold bars of the headboard feeling trapped like White Bird must have felt in his gold cage, only she's trapped in a condominium cage. "I don't care, Momma. I'm glad I let him go. One of us needs to be free."

A flicker of light in her black lacquer mirror catches her eye. The man Daddy brought that mirror from in Japan said it was a magic mirror, and it's true. That's where she found Mim, her only friend in the whole world. Maybe Mim can tell her what to say to Daddy if he asks about White Bird.

She runs to the mirror and kneels down. "I'm scared, Mim. I did something I shouldn't have done."

Mim touches her fingers through the glass. She looks worried.

"It wasn't my fault, Mim. I had to do it. I had to let White Bird go."

Mim's eyes say that might not be true.

"Honestly, Mim. I didn't know what else to do. White Bird was so sad, I thought he would die."

Mim still looks unsure.

Maddie wants to convince her, but she hears voices downstairs. That means Daddy's home.

She runs to the door and presses her ear against the wood, trying to hear what they're saying. Daddy's voice comes through like the whooshing wings of a raven flying through a forest, dodging trees.

Momma squawks. Is she telling Daddy what a bad girl he has? That's not right. She was just trying to keep White Bird from dying. She shouldn't be blamed for that.

She goes out and sits on the top step where she can hear their actual words. She's above the curve of the stairs, so she can't see Momma, but she can see Daddy at the balcony window, staring out into the night.

Momma squawks, "That's right, Mister Big Man! Blame it on me. Your precious Maddie lets the bird out, and somehow it's my fault."

Daddy lifts a shoulder and lets it drop in a sad way. "Well, you *were* the adult in the house."

"Right. The only adult. But believe me, Maddie's smarter than you know. She may be seven, going on eight, but she's got the mind of a twenty-year-old. It's all those books you keep bringing her."

Daddy glances back. "That's what books are for, dear. To make you older and wiser. You should read one sometime."

"Well, Mr. Smarty Pants, I'm sick of it. I'm not going to spend the rest of my life trapped in this damn condo keeping an eye on her while you fly around the world."

Daddy sighs. "Is that right?"

"Yes. That's right."

Maddie can't believe it. Is Momma really going to stop keeping an eye on her? Will she be able to go down to the playground to swing with the boys? Will she be able to climb the maple trees along the sidewalk and maybe find White Bird and fly away with him?

She scoots down a step to where she can see Momma on the sofa showing off her pretty legs like she does when she wants to change Daddy's mood.

It's not going to work this time. Daddy can't see it. He's still at the window staring out.

He glances back at the empty bird cage in the corner and lets out another long sigh, like he's frustrated, or probably disappointed. "Well," he says, "it's too bad we lost the bird." He turns back to the window, lifts his shoulder again, and lets it drop. "So, will we be having dinner tonight?"

"I don't know anything about dinner, dear. Didn't you bring it?" Now Momma's voice is low and murmuring. She lets her robe slip off one shoulder, lifts her blond curls, and lets them tumble down like a waterfall. She smiles, her eyes shining emerald-green for him.

Daddy doesn't see any of it.

He sighs and turns from the window to answer Momma's question. "No, actually, dear, I didn't bring dinner. Maybe you could scramble up some eggs or something while I change my clothes. It's been a long day. I'm tired and hungry. Where's Maddie?"

"In her room, where I sent her."

Daddy heads for the stairs.

Maddie races to her room and shuts the door. When she thinks he's had time to reach the top step, she opens the door and whispers, "Hi, Daddy. I'm glad you're home."

He comes and tousles her hair. "Hi, Maddie, girl. I hear you let the bird go today. Why'd you do that?"

"I'm sorry, Daddy. I really am. It's just that he was so sad. He wouldn't eat, drink, or sing. He wouldn't do anything. I thought he might die."

"Is that right?"

"Yes. I thought if I let him out for a minute it would help. He could fly around and feel free, then he'd go back in his cage. But he went crazy. Like the room was too small. He crashed into the walls and the ceiling. Before I could catch him, he flew out the window. He kept flying back to me, cawing really loud, like he wanted me to go with him. So I did. I went flying with White Bird, Daddy. We were like Peter Pan. It was really fun." She slaps her hand over her mouth. She wasn't supposed to tell him about flying.

Daddy looks shocked.

"It's okay, Daddy. I landed in the flowers. It was soft. I didn't get hurt at all." She holds out her arms to show him.

He puts his hands on her shoulders. "The flowers? What flowers? What are you saying?"

Why is he so upset? It's not her fault. "White Bird made me do it, Daddy. He kept coming back, squawking so loud, I had to go with him. We went flying, and I landed in the flowers, and that's when Gardener came."

Daddy keeps his hands on her shoulders and looks deep into her eyes like he's trying to see if she's lying, but she'd never lie to Daddy. She loves him too much. Doesn't he know that?

He shakes his head and heads back downstairs.

She follows him to the kitchen where he backs Momma into the corner. "I thought you said Gardener tried to get the bird back. You didn't say he found Maddie in the flowerbed. What does she mean, she landed in the flowers?"

Momma's eyes turn dark. "What'd you say, Maddie? What kind of lies have you been telling?"

"I didn't lie, Momma! I just told him I went flying with White Bird, that I landed in the flowers, and Gardener brought me up here, where you hurt my head with your hard kisses." She looks to Daddy for help. "I don't like Momma's hard kisses. Please, Daddy, tell her to not do it."

He shakes his head like he can't believe what he's hearing. "Is it true? Our Maddie went off the balcony after the bird? Seven stories high? Is that what happened?"

Momma tosses her blond curls and scoffs. "That's crazy. How could she survive such a fall?"

What Momma's saying isn't true. "I didn't fall, Daddy. I went flying. I landed in the flowers, and I didn't get hurt at all. It was fun, and I want to do it again. Can I, Daddy? Can I?"

Momma throws up her black kimono wings and lets out a red-tailed-hawk squawk. "Of course, she didn't go off the balcony? It's just another one of her fairytale fantasies. It's a lie."

Momma storms out of the kitchen and hurries upstairs to her bedroom to her whiskey. Maddie knows it's true. That's what she always does when she can't think of anything to say.

That's okay with Maddie. She wants to be alone with Daddy.

He takes her hand, pulls her into the living room, and gently presses her down into the black leather chair. He walks back and forth in front of her, loosening his tie, looking worried. He stops in front of her and shakes his head. "What am I going to do with you, Maddie?"

She shrugs and tries to smile. "I don't know. Why do you have to do anything?"

"You keep making things up. You live in a fantasy world of Peter Pan and *Alice in Wonderland*. Those people aren't real, Maddie. Neverland doesn't exist. It's just a made-up place in one of your books."

"I'm not making things up about White Bird. Momma told me not to tell you, but I want you to know I went flying. I like flying, Daddy. I really do. If White Bird comes back, he can teach me to fly better, so I can land in the top of the trees instead of in the flowers. Then, I'll never get hurt. I can land wherever I want to."

Daddy kneels in front of her chair and cradles her head in his hands. He rests his head against her forehead, so she feels the heavy, sad weight of it.

"I'm sorry, Daddy. I wasn't trying to make you sad."

He sits back on his heels and looks at her with a half smile. "You've got to stop this, Maddie. Do you hear me? You've got to come out and live in the real world."

She slugs the padded arms of the chair. "I don't have a real world, Daddy! I live inside this condominium cage! I don't have any friends. I can't go anywhere or see anything, all because Momma's scared. I can't even go to school. Nothing ever happens here, Daddy. I'm dying of boredom and loneliness."

"I know. I know. But Momma can't help it. She has real reasons for being scared."

"What reasons?"

"I promise, I'll tell you some day, but not now." He stands and goes back to the balcony window and stares out into the dark for a long time.

He must be looking for White Bird.

Maddie runs to his side and points to the sky. "White Bird went that way, Daddy, toward that blue star. Don't you love the night sky? The stars, the colorful city lights: the blue and green. The red and the shimmering gold."

"Yes, honey, it's beautiful."

He goes silent for a while, then touches her shoulder. "Hey, I've got an idea."

"You do?"

"Yes. I do. I think what you need is a tutor."

"A tutor?"

"Yes. A teacher who can see the spark of your intelligence and find a way to nurture it. Someone who'll come on weekdays, so you don't get so lonely and bored."

Maddie grabs his hand and kisses it. "Oh, Daddy. I'd love that so much. Can I really have a tutor?"

"Yes. I think that's exactly what you need. You've taken in all my lessons and stories and devoured every book I've brought home. What you need now is someone who can help you integrate all that knowledge so you can think for yourself. I believe I know just the person who can do that."

Maddie can hardly believe it. "Oh boy. What kind of things will I learn?"

He smiles and shrugs. "I don't know. Everything, I guess. Why not? You've got an exceptional mind. Like Momma said, you're an eight-year-old going on twenty, but I think I know a young man smart enough to stay ahead of you." He looks deep into her eyes again "So, you'd like a tutor, huh?"

She shouts, "Yes, Daddy! Get him here as fast as you can. But please, don't tell Momma. She'll just get scared and try to stop you."

Chapter 3

Maddie flips through her closet looking for something pretty to wear. Her Tutor's coming today. She needs to look her very best. She'd wear her white princess dress, but it's dirty from flying with White Bird. If Momma sees it, she'll send it to the cleaners, and all her flying memories will be washed away.

She hides her princess dress in the back of the closet and takes out her purple and pink paisley dress. She holds it up and twirls over to the mirror to show Mim.

Mim smiles and nods.

"Oh good. I like it too." Maddie slips the dress over her head and kneels with her nose against Mim's nose, feeling the cool slickness of the glass between them. "I wish you could meet my Tutor, Mim."

Mim looks sad, but then her eyes shine.

Maddie knows what that means. "That's right. You can meet him once we're sure we can trust him."

They touch foreheads and make the low, sighing sound of an owl as it takes flight, their oath to keep their friendship secret.

Maddie runs downstairs and finds Momma and Daddy at the kitchen table having their morning coffee. Daddy's got his dark gray work suit on. Momma's wearing her pale blue linen pantsuit with a soft white satin blouse. She must want to look her best for Tutor too.

She gives Momma a quick kiss on the cheek and twirls around the table to curtsy for Daddy, hoping he'll notice her dress.

He smiles "Good morning, Maddie. You look lovely. How'd you sleep?"

"I didn't sleep at all, Daddy. I was too...excited."

Momma plunks her coffee cup on the glass table and scowls at Daddy like he's done something wrong. "Are you sure about this?"

Daddy shakes his head with frustration. "Look, we've been through this. Maddie needs a tutor. There are things she needs to understand about the world that she can't get from books or from us. We agreed on that."

Momma lifts her hair and narrows her green eyes. "Yes, I agreed to that, but she doesn't need to learn from a boy. You should have found a young woman to teach her."

Daddy throws up his hands. "Look, it's done. And he's not a boy, he's a young man, not that much younger than you. He has a master's degree in philosophy and psychology. He's interesting and smart. He's fun and creative, and he's experienced some sadness in his own life, which has given him the ability to empathize with others. Who could be more qualified to teach our Maddie?"

Momma scoffs. "How do you know all that?"

"I just do. Now, why don't you fix Maddie some breakfast before he arrives."

Maddie grabs his arm. "I can't eat, Daddy. My stomach's too full of butterflies."

"Well, at least have some juice or something." He goes to the refrigerator, pours her a tall glass of orange juice, and sets it down on the table. "Here. Drink this."

She can't even think of drinking juice right now, but Daddy wants her to do it, so she takes a big gulp. The doorbell chimes before she can swallow. She spits the juice back in the glass and looks at Daddy to see if she should go answer the door.

He says, "I'll get it, but come with me, if you like."

When Daddy opens the door, Maddie gasps. Her Tutor isn't anything like she imagined He's wearing a black magician's suit, a Mad Hatter top hat, and glittery red shoes, like Dorothy's in the *Wizard of Oz*. His hair is shiny black, with a thin mustache and a little pointed beard on the tip of his chin that she really likes. But the most surprising thing is his eyes. How can anyone's eyes be that turquoise blue?

Daddy touches her shoulder. "Tutor, this is our Maddie."

She holds out her hand. "It's very nice to meet you, Tutor. I'm so glad you're here."

Tutor dips his head and smiles. "It's very nice to meet you too, Miss Maddie." He shakes her hand, then reaches up quickly and pulls a coin from her ear. Holding it in the palm of his hand, he offers it to her.

She grabs it, thinking, Oh boy, he really is a magician. Is he going to teach her how to do magic? That would be so great.

She holds up the coin and rubs it between her fingers, admiring the shine. "Look, Daddy. It's pure gold. Can I keep it?"

He shares a smile with Tutor and says, "Sure. Why not?"

Momma comes out of the kitchen with a frown and puts an end to the magic.

Tutor holds out his hand. "It's very nice to meet you, Missus."

Momma steps back, like she's seen a snake. She turns on her heels and heads upstairs without a word.

Daddy looks worried for a minute, then shakes it off and smiles. "Okay, you two, follow me. I'll show you where these lessons will take place."

They go to the study. Daddy closes the door and gives Tutor a serious look. "Like I said, I want you to teach our Maddie how to think. I mean, deeply. About everything. You're up to that, right?"

Tutor tips his top hat and bows with a flourish. "Of course. It would be my pleasure, Big Daddy."

Daddy chuckles and turns serious again. "Don't forget her imagination. You understand? We don't want her to lose that."

"No, Sir. She'll need her imagination. I promise to take good care of that. You might say, that's my area of expertise." He twirls his hat on his finger and makes it disappear. No, it didn't disappear, but it could have in a magic world.

Daddy chuckles again and looks back and forth between them. "Okay then. I'm off to the office. You two have fun." He reaches for the doorknob and turns back to Tutor. "Just so you know, you can lock this door from the inside, if needs be."

Tutor raises an eyebrow.

"I mean, if you get any unwarranted interruptions. It's okay to say no to that."

Maddie knows he means if Momma tries to come in, and she probably will. She always wants to be in charge of everything when Daddy's not home. But this time, they can keep her out. That's good.

When Daddy leaves, Tutor walks around the study looking at everything. Maddie walks around too. She loves Daddy's study so much. His big mahogany desk, the black lacquer bookshelves along the wall, the soft black leather chairs with wheels, one on Daddy's side of the desk and two on the other side for visitors, if they ever came. But they don't.

That's okay. She and Tutor can use those chairs.

She goes to the tall Japanese vase in the corner, it's shiny black, with a mother-of-pearl peacock spreading his white tail under a shimmering full moon. She loves that vase, especially now that she knows about the white peacock on Enoshima Island. It has to be the same peacock. She presses her ear against the vase, hoping to hear the whispering Buddha.

She can't.

It feels like Tutor is watching her. She turns to see if it's true. No, he's not watching her. He's looking through Daddy's books on world history and science. His Audubon books and the ones about great artists. There are a lot of wonderful things in Daddy's study, and what she loves best is that it's not like the other rooms, which are too bright and too full of things with hard edges that bruise her legs if she's not careful. She doesn't like being careful.

She squishes her toes into the thick blue softness of the Chinese rug with the flying white horse. That horse might give her another way to fly , even though she promised Momma she wouldn't .

Now, Tutor's looking at Daddy's stained-glass lamp. She hurries to his side. "I love that lamp, Tutor. See how pure the color of the fruit is. The cherry red apples. The yellow lemons. The violet grapes."

He tips his head. "Violet, huh? Why not purple?"

She shrugs. "I like violet more."

"Why's that?"

"Well, it's more inbetween. I mean, it's not dark like purple. Violet has more light than purple, light, like a feather. I like feathers, Tutor. And birds. I like birds so much."

He clicks his red heels and salutes her. "Oh, that's good, Maddie. That's so good. I like a girl with a mind that can travel to the inbetween places. You know, not everyone can do that. Most people prefer solid ground. They want a world with perfectly defined opposites. True and false. Right and wrong. A world without...ambiguity."

Maddie doesn't know what that word means, but she loves that he likes her mind.

"Anyways, I think we're going to get on famously." He squints with one eye. "You know, until just now, I wondered if we'd have a single thing to say to each other. I mean, I'm not that old, but I'm not that young either. What *is* our age difference?" He looks at her, rocking his head back and forth, trying to guess. "What's the difference between twenty-six and...how old are you?"

"Almost eight."

"Okay, what's the difference between twenty-six and eight."

Maddie works it out in her head. "Eighteen. Right?"

"Yes. Quite right."

She frowns. "That's a lot of difference, isn't it?"

"Nah, not so much. I can see you're growing up fast. And me, I just keep getting younger."

He smiles and looks back at the lamp. "You're right about the colors. Fruit colors, yes, but they can also be seen as pure color. Yellow and red, which are primary colors. Violet, a secondary color composed of magenta and blue. There's no need for further abstraction once you've defined them as color."

Maddie frowns. "I don't know what that word means, Tutor. Can you tell me?"

"Abstraction?"

She nods.

"Sure. There are some things, like colors that are just what they are. We engage the color directly with our senses and give it a name, like blue or orange. But thinking, in the way Big Daddy wants you to think, requires abstraction. You know, using concepts and abstractions that allow you to see colors in various ways. For example, the opposite qualities of black and white, the warmth of red, the coolness of blue.

He scratches his head. "Anyways, just let me say that once you learn how to think abstractly, with concepts, you won't be weighed down by all the minutia. You know, the details and facts. The more concepts you have in your mind, the faster you'll be able to fly through the realm of ideas, changing the world as you go. That's what we're here to do. Right?" He pauses. "Do you understand what I'm trying to say, Maddie. Do you see why it's important to be able to think abstractly?"

She takes a deep breath and lets it out quick. "I don't know about that, but I do know how to fly. I flew with White Bird." She claps her hand over her mouth, wishing she hadn't said that.

Tutor flaps his elbows like a bird and giggles.

She flaps her elbow wings too, and pretty soon they're both giggling so hard, it makes her stomach hurt. She gasps, "What's so funny, Tutor?"

"Not funny, Maddie. Glorious. That's what you are. You've got a beautiful mind. I can see that already. We're going to have a grand old time learning together. And, someday, when you're ready, I'd like to hear more about your flight with that White Bird."

He twirls over to the big world map on the wall next to the blackboard and runs his finger across the different colors of the countries, saying, "Oh yes, this will do nicely."

He looks back at her. "Okay, *Maddie*. If you want to be a thinking person, you'll need to understand the basic concepts of a lot of subjects, subjects like geography, history, politics...war. Yes, war. You can learn a lot from war. You'll also need to understand the social sciences, sociology, philosophy, psychology. Linguistics. You might even want to know physics, though I don't."

He lifts his hands. "You see, every area of knowledge has its own set of rules. Its own vocabulary and unique set of concepts that let you see the world in a particular way."

She smiles and nods, hoping he'll think she understands.

He shakes his head at the floor. "I'm sorry. I'm getting ahead of myself. I haven't really done this before. We're going to have to find our way. Just know, Maddie, I'll get you to where you understand what I'm saying. Then, I'll show you so many different versions of the world, it'll make your head spin. And while it's spinning, you'll be thinking like Big Daddy wants you to think. You'll be perceiving the simplicity *and* the deep complexity of things, simultaneously. That is, at the same time. You'll discover the patterns and possibilities in each conceptual view. Hold onto that thought, Maddie. I'll get you there as soon as I can."

"I'll try to hold it, Tutor, but I don't know exactly what I'm supposed to hold."

"Good point. What is *it*? I guess you could say *it's* your mind. I mean, the more concepts you have in your mind, the wider and richer your perception of the world will be. And why wouldn't everyone want that? I can assure you, living in a rich world of endless possibilities is marvelous. A real hoot!"

He toots an imaginary horn, then rolls one of the black leather chairs closer to the blackboard. "Okay then, why don't you sit there, and let's get started."

Chapter 4

Tutor paces for a minute, then gives her a look like he's trying to decide how much she can understand. He takes a deep breath and closes his eyes, which gives Maddie a chance to look him over more closely. She's never seen anyone like Tutor, not even on TV. His face changes so fast from serious to silly, it's like he's a character from one of her fairytale books. Or maybe he slipped out of her magic mirror in the middle of the night. She'll have to ask Mim about that.

He opens his eyes, spins his hat on his finger, and tosses it across the room to the top rung of Daddy's antique coat rack in the corner.

Maddie gasps. "How'd you do that?"

He gives her a look like he doesn't have a clue what she's talking about. Then he twirls across the room with sparks shooting out from his red Dorothy shoes. "Anyways . . .I guess before we get into more complex concepts, we should get opposites out of the way."

"You mean opposites like up and down?"

"That'll work." He goes to the blackboard and draws a tall vertical line. He writes the word *up* at the top of the line, and *down* at the bottom, and comes back to her. "Okay. The important thing to know is that opposites are a basic concept for organizing and understanding the world we live in. I mean, if we're walking down the street and we come to a crossroads, we use directional opposites, like

North and South or Left and Right, to decide which way to go. We rely on an internal map shaped by past experience, or we consult an actual map to see what lies in each direction before making our choice. Sometimes, we don't know what each choice holds, but we still have to choose. Otherwise, we'll be stuck where we are." He glances away, looking sheepish, and clears his throat. "Anyways, you see how humans use opposites to navigate the world? Right?"

Maddie tries to think back to when he started talking to see if she can figure out how to answer his question. She can't do it, so she just says, "Uh huh."

He taps the vertical line he drew on the blackboard with chalk. "Okay then, let's talk about up and down. Up and down are pretty straightforward concepts, wouldn't you say?"

Maddie shrugs. "I'm not sure what that means."

He comes closer. "I mean, up is everything above the level of down, and down is everything below the level of up. There's no question about that, is there?"

"I guess not."

"Now…" he swivels his hips on the way back to the blackboard and draws a long, sloping line from one side of the board to the other. He writes *up* on the high end of the line and *down* on the low end and looks back. "…if we draw a diagonal line, we can talk about more abstract concepts such as elevation and slope." He lets out a groan. "Well, we *could* do that, but slope gets us into algebra, and that's a little abstract for where we are right now."

Maddie stares at him, trying not to shake her head in confusion. How can he think she has any idea what he's saying? Does he think she's a genius?

He looks at her and smacks his forehead. "Sorry, Maddie. I tend to get a bit…tangential at times. I'll get back to my point." He puffs up his cheeks and exhales, sending out a swirl of glittery blue light. "So, what other opposites do you know?"

She thinks about it. "Well…there's black and white. And good and bad. And—"

His eyes sparkle. "Oh, yes. I can see you know exactly where I'm going."

"I do?"

"Most definitely." He erases his sloping line and adds *white* and *good* next to *up* at the top of his first line, and *black* and *bad* at the bottom of the line, next to *down*. He steps aside and looks back at Maddie. "Remember how I said most people don't like living in the inbetween worlds."

She nods.

"How they prefer the absolute world of black and white, or good and bad, and can't see that those are just the extremes of the equation." His face turns serious. "Look at all this gray area between the two extremes, Maddie." He screeches his chalk back and forth across the middle part of his up and down line.

Maddie stares at the blackboard and back at Tutor wondering what she's supposed to see. She's about to ask when she thinks of another pair of opposites he might like. "What about heaven and hell, Tutor? Do they work?"

He claps his hands and gets on one knee in front of her like he's the prince that wants to marry her. "Oh, Maddie. You're so good."

She blushes and tries to remember what she said, but she can't.

He gets up and returns to the blackboard to add *heaven* at the top of his line and *hell* at the bottom. "Do you see what you've done?"

"Not really, Tutor. Is it good?"

"I'll say. And I mean *good* in a very good way." He lets out a little giggle and turns serious again. "So, Maddie, let's look at black and white. It's pretty clear what each word means, and why they're opposites, right?"

"Yes. They're both colors that almost aren't colors. Just dark and light. The thing that makes something seem heavy, or light and feathery, like a bird."

His eyes twinkle bright blue. "What else?"

She thinks. "Well, black can be *exciting* too. Like at night, when it's all black and quiet and the stars and lights come out on all the buildings and sparkle with different colors. That doesn't work in the white light of day, but then, that's when the birds sing in the trees, and them being quiet or noisy are opposites too."

"Yes! What else? What about good and bad? What do you think of that pair of opposites?" He rolls over Daddy's other black leather chair and sits down. When he swivels the chair to face her, a hot spark jumps between their knees.

She flips the hair off her neck to cool off and tries to answer his question. "Well, I guess *good* and *bad* are different from the other opposites."

"Why's that?"

"Umm...because you can be punished for being bad. And if you're good, nobody will even notice. Anyway, that's how Momma is." She slaps her hand over her mouth. She doesn't want to think about Momma right now.

Tutor nods with understanding in his eyes. "I can see that disturbs you. Now why do you think some sets of opposites create that kind of strong feeling? The opposites of *up* and *down* don't do that. Right?"

"Well, only if you live *up* in a seventh floor condo and you want to go *down* to the playground to swing with the boys, but you can't, because—"

Tutor's eyes soften. "Because why?"

"Because going down there is *bad*. At least, that's what *some* people think. But I don't understand why I have to be the only one up here, while the other kids get to be down in the park swinging so high they're almost like birds. I want to fly like a bird, Tutor. I know how. So, why can't I?"

That seems to make Tutor sad. She doesn't want him to be sad. It's just that his lesson made her think about things she hasn't had anyone to talk to about, except Mim, and Mim never responds, except with her eyes. Tutor's so fun and easy to talk to. And he's right here. Why did she have to go and make him sad? She rocks her head back and forth in a silly way, hoping to make him smile.

He *does* smile, then he pulls his glossy black hair up into a spiky peak. "Anyways…where were we?"

"Um…I think we were talking about good and bad, and I got lost talking about some other things. I'm sorry."

"It's okay, Maddie. It was a good example of what I'm trying to teach you." He gives her a look that makes that hot white spark from before jump between their eyes. She tries to look away, but she can't.

"Think about it, Maddie. Up and down are pure. Like those colors in Big Daddy's lamp. Up and down mean just what they mean. It's only life experience, like yours, that makes that basic meaning go all…wobbly." He wobbles his body to match his word.

Maddie claps. "Oh, Tutor, you're so funny. I love you."

He dips his head, "Why *thank* you, Miss Maddie. I love you too." He tilts his head right, then left. "Yes, love and hate. An interesting pair of opposites. We'll cover all that later. Right now, if you don't mind, let's get back to our world of concepts."

She still doesn't know what that word *concept* means, but she doesn't care. She just wants to hear what he's going to say next.

He jumps up, goes to the blackboard, and looks back over his shoulder. "So, Maddie. Why do you think *good* and *bad* and *heaven* and *hell* are so different, in most cases, from *up* and *down* and *black* and *white*?"

"Uh…maybe because there's *trouble* inside them? I mean, people want to be good because they're supposed to be good, but sometimes they can't help being bad."

"And who gets to decide what's good and bad?"

She punches the padded arms of the chair. "Momma! She's always the one."

"And what about Big Daddy?"

She shrugs. "Well, I guess he decides things too. I mean, Momma wants to move back to Littletown, but Daddy can't live there because of his work, so she can't either."

Tutor comes over and looks deep into her eyes. "Okay, then, if Momma decides what's good and bad, who gets to decide whether you go to heaven or hell?"

She stares at him, not sure. "I guess God gets to decide that, but I don't know very much about God. I mean, I don't know if he's real or not. Momma might think he's real, but Daddy doesn't. I think the angels are real, because, sometimes…well, it just seems like they are. And, sometimes, devils seem real too."

Tutor sits down. "Why's that?"

"The part about devils being real?"

"Yes. That part."

"Well, sometimes when I read books, the bad people seem really bad and mean, almost like devils. I mean, that's how the Bad Wolf is in *Little Red Riding Hood*. He's really mean. He ate the grandmother, and then he wants to eat the girl, but she can see he has big ears, and big eyes, and his teeth look scary, so she's careful." She takes a breath.

"And what about the Wicked Stepmother and her daughter in *East of the Sun and West of the Moon*? They were the ones who placed the curse that turned the prince into a white bear. The girl was warned not to look at him while he slept, but her mother convinced her to do it. When she lit the candle, she saw that he was a handsome prince, but in her surprise, she accidentally spilled wax onto his shirt. That's why he was forced to return to the stepmother's castle, where he would have to marry her daughter, unless the girl could find a way to save him."

She takes another quick breath and continues, "The girl made a mistake by looking at the bear and trying to kiss him, but she wasn't mean. The stepmother and her daughter were the mean ones for making the curse in the first place."

Maddie thinks about Momma and how mean she is, always telling her to stop doing whatever she's doing, especially when she's been drinking whiskey, which is almost all of the time now. Momma cries sometimes, saying she can't live in the city, that she'll die if she can't go back to Littletown, where she feels safe. Maddie wishes she knew why Momma was so scared all the time.

Tutor's looking at her in a strange way. "Where'd you go, Maddie. Off on some flight of fancy?"

"Is that what it's called."

"I can't say for sure, but what a beautiful understanding you have of the fairytale people. Your mind is fascinating, the way you put this and that together, pulling ideas into the inbetween world." He runs his fingers through his hair and smiles. "You sound like you've read a lot of books and have done a fair amount of thinking about those books."

"It's true, Tutor. Daddy brings me new books all the time, and there are a lot of books here in the study, and some on my bookshelf. I read them during the day and think about them at night. There's nothing else to do, except, sometimes, I talk to Mim."

"Mim?" Tutor's eyes spark with interest.

"Maddie in the Mirror, I mean–" She slaps her hand over her mouth. She's never told anyone about Mim, not even Daddy. Now, Tutor is going to want to know who Mim is, and she's going to have to break their oath not to tell anyone. She closes her eyes and whispers, "I'm sorry, Mim. I'm sorry." She squeezes the arms of the chair, keeping her eyes closed.

Tutor touches her arm. "It's okay, Maddie. I didn't hear a thing. Your promise is as good as gold. I promise."

She knows he's telling the truth by the seriousness in his eyes. It makes her want to tell him about Mim, but right now she wants to ask him something she's been wondering about. "Tutor. Do you think grown-ups can be lonely?"

"Sure. They're people too, aren't they?"

"I think Momma's lonely. That's why she's mean sometimes. She's not really a devil."

Tutor frowns. "She doesn't hurt you, does she?"

"No. Never. She just...well, sometimes, she doesn't mean to, but—I don't want to talk about it."

"You said she's lonely? Doesn't she have friends?"

"I guess she does, back in Littletown."

"You mentioned Littletown before. Where is that?"

"It's where Momma lived before she met Daddy and fell in love. He brought her back to the city, but now Momma hates the city. She's afraid of everything here. She wants to live in Littletown, but Daddy's never going to go there. He has his work here, and he likes the city, and I was just wondering if that's why she's so upset and mean sometimes. Maybe she's just lonely, like White Bird was before I let him go free, and like I was, before you came."

Tutor looks sad again. "So far, you've said your Momma's lonely and scared and sometimes she's angry and mean. You know, Maddie. Most people are how they are because of things that have happened throughout their life. They follow a path from one experience to the next, until they arrive right where they are. Sometimes that leads a person to a sad place. They believe the world is exactly as they perceive it to be. They can't get free of that, so they can't change. If they could see the relationship between what exists in their mind and the world they perceive, just knowing *that* would give them a degree of freedom. I want you to have that kind of freedom, Maddie. I want to give you a basket full of perceptual options, which will allow you to decide who you want to be and what kind of world you want to live in."

She wants to ask how she can be free right now, but Tutor's headed back to the blackboard. He adds *right* and *wrong* to his list of opposites and turns back. "So, what do you think about right and wrong?"

"Aren't they the same as good and bad?"

"Not quite. Good and bad are more a *personal* measure of something an individual likes or dislikes, whereas right and wrong are determined by a *consensus,* or an *agreement,* among people who live together in a social or religious group. The rules, or laws, of right and wrong, are designed to keep things from getting too chaotic. If you step beyond what your society considers legally wrong, you can be fined, jailed, or even executed, if the wrong is great enough. Are you with me, Maddie?"

"Uh...I'm not sure."

"I'm sorry. I'm talking about the *laws* associated with right and wrong. You know, laws about stealing, and killing, and cheating on your taxes."

"My *taxes*?"

He frowns. "Well, not *your* taxes. I mean the kind of things a society decides people can't get away with because it would cause too much harm to everyone else. You know, like stealing and murder?"

"Am I going to have a test on this, Tutor?"

"No. No. I don't believe in tests. They force you into believing there's only one right answer to a question, and that's never true." He runs his finger down his nose, over his lips, to his chin. He tugs on his little black beard and turns away.

That worries Maddie. Maybe he doesn't think she's smart enough to learn. She jumps up runs to his side. "It's okay, Tutor. If you're patient, I'll be able to understand. I promise."

Now, there's a soft smile on his face, and his eyes are the luminous turquoise blue of a Robin's egg. "I know you will, Maddie. We'll find our way. That's my promise to you."

They go back to the leather chairs and sit down. Tutor crosses his legs in a tall way. "Maybe I should get straight to the point."

"Okay." Maddie crosses her legs in the same tall way.

"I'm trying to show you how opposites can be used to create rules and laws for us to live by, which is a good thing, right?"

"It seems right."

"It's a good thing because it helps people live together and get along. But opposites can also be used by people who want to have control over you for their own purposes. Momma has power over you, right? She gets to decide what's good and what's bad. But she's your Momma, so she needs to do that, to some extent, so you'll grow up knowing things you need to know to keep yourself safe along the way. Isn't that right?"

"Yes, but sometimes she says things are bad when they really *aren't*, so what should I do then?"

"Exactly."

Tutor's eyes shine in a way that tells her she's said something good again. She rubs the smooth leather of the chair feeling warm and safe in a way she hasn't felt in a long time, except with Daddy, sometimes.

"Maddie, I'm sorry to tell you, but some people take advantage of the power they have to say what's good and what's bad. What's right and wrong. They might decide things in an arbitrary and unwise way, just so they can feel their own power. Other people might want to be in charge of right and wrong because they truly believe they know how we're supposed to behave. They want everyone to submit to their version of truth because they believe it will make them happy, or keep them safe, or get them to heaven. Or maybe, they just want the power of being in charge of reality. Momma probably has a good reason for keeping you away from the swings. Maybe she thinks they're dangerous, and she's trying to protect you."

"No! It's because she's a big scaredy-cat, so she wants me to be scardey-cat too. She wants to be safe back in Little-town with the cows and the chickens and pigs. But it's not my fault she has to stay in the city."

"No, it's not your fault, Maddie. Do you know what she's afraid of?"

"No. But Daddy told me something bad happened to her, and that he'll tell me about, but not now. I think it was when I was little, and she's been that way ever since. It seems like we used to have fun. Sometimes we'd be silly or we'd play charades and sing songs together. Sometimes Momma and Daddy would dance, but I'm not sure if any of that's true. Maybe it was just a dream I had."

Tutor looks troubled. "I wonder what happened to create such fear in your Momma."

"I don't know. One time, I heard Daddy tell her it won't happen again and it wasn't her fault. She yelled, 'You don't know whose fault it was. You don't know if it will happen again. You weren't there. You're never here.' It was like she was blaming Daddy for what happened, but she was blaming herself too."

Tutor meets her eyes. "And you don't have any idea what they were talking about?"

"No. I just know that she's scared all the time, and she won't go down into the city, even when Daddy asks her really nice for a date. She won't let me go anywhere either."

"It must be frustrating not to be able to help her, but you can't do much if you don't know what's causing her fear."

"It's true, Tutor. I'd like to help, but I don't know what's wrong."

He gives her a sad smile. "Well, it sounds like someday Big Daddy will tell you what happened. Until then, all you can do is try to help her feel happy and safe."

"I'll try, Tutor. I promise. I wish Momma could be as happy as I am now that you're here. I've been so lonely. That's part of the reason I went flying with White Bird, and the reason you're here. It made Daddy decide I needed a tutor, and now, here you are, and I'm so glad."

"Well, that's good then, isn't it? See how things work out? One thing leading to the next and the next and the next until we end up right where we are. By the way, you said something about that White Bird before. Did you really go flying?"

"I really did. White Bird taught me how to do it. Do you know how to fly?"

He jumps up, twiddles his little beard, and crosses his eyes making them jiggle in a funny way. "Well, my dear, it depends on what you mean by flying. Are you speaking literally or figuratively?"

"You know. Flying like a bird does. With wings. Flying so high you can look down on all the little people on the sidewalk. Sometimes when you fly in dreams, you end up so high you're above the clouds. You can fly all the way to Neverland, if you want to."

"Peter Pan, huh?"

"Yes!" Maddie shouts. "Peter Pan. Do you know him?"

"*Know* him? I *am* him." He shines his blue eyes and points to the sky. "Second star to the right and straight on 'til morning."

Maddie shouts. "You really *are* Peter Pan."

"Sure. Didn't you know? Me and Tinker Bell go flying all the time."

Maddie snickers. "I thought maybe you were one of those other ones, you know, like Ali Baba. But I hope not. Everyone wants to hurt him. Don't be Ali Baba, okay?"

Tutor frowns and shakes his head, making a sound like clinking coins. "No. Not Ali Baba, more like The Mad Hatter, if you ask me. You know the Mad Hatter, right?"

"Of course, I do. Sometimes I feel like Alice is my sister. If I had any sisters. If I had *anyone*."

Tutor's eyes turn sad again. "I know what you mean."

"You do?"

"Yes. I'm an only one too."

"You are?"

"Yep. Just me. Alone in the world."

"Really, Tutor? You don't have any family or friends?"

His eyes shimmer. "Well, now, I have you."

"You really do, Tutor. And you know what? I'll be your little sister, if you want me to."

"That would be marvelous, Maddie. Guess that means I'd be your big brother."

She jumps up. "Should we make a blood oath."

"Sure. How does it go?"

She stands in front of his chair, takes his hand, and pretends to draw blood by pulling her fingernails across his wrist. Tutor does the same to her. They press their wrists together, and she feels the warmth of their blood mixing. She whispers, "I promise to be your sister forever." She makes the sound of the sighing owl as it takes flight, and waits for Tutor to do it.

Tutor whispers, "I promise to be your brother, Maddie. I promise to be your friend and keep an eye out for you at all times." There's a dark seriousness in his eyes that tells her it's a real promise that he'll keep forever, even if he didn't make the sound of the sighing owl. That doesn't matter. They mixed their blood.

She holds his hand to her cheek. "I've never had a brother before. I've never had a single friend, except... White Bird, and he's gone. Other than that, I've only had Momma and Daddy. And Gardener, of course, but he mostly stays in the garden. And there's Granny, but she died. And Maid comes to clean the house, but she speaks with different words, so I don't know what she's saying most of the time."

"Don't you ever go to the movies, Maddie. Haven't you ever seen a play?"

"I watch movies on Momma's TV, but it's in her bedroom, and she gets to decide which shows we watch. I saw the movie about the boy and girl that were trapped on the island. They built a tree house and lived there until somebody came to save them. I'd love to live in a tree with the birds. I wouldn't care if they came to save me or not."

"If you like trees and birds, maybe you wouldn't mind living in Littletown with Momma. How do you feel about chickens?"

Maddie kicks out her foot. "I don't like chickens. They're mean, like little devils. When we were in Littletown watching Granny die, they chased me around trying to peck my legs."

Tutor scratches his foot on the floor like he's got chicken claws, then he bends his elbows and wiggles them like wings. "You've just got to learn how to speak chicken." He struts around clucking and making other chicken sounds.

Maddie giggles. "What did you just say to the chickens?"

"I said, calm down. We're just visiting from the big city for a few days. No need to get yourself in a lather."

Maddie laughs. "Do you think it'll work?"

"Who knows, but we might as well try. You can't hurt a chicken by talking to it."

"Well, it might hurt *you* if it pecks your legs."

"You're a funny girl, Maddie."

"I am?"

"Yep."

"You're funny too, Tutor."

"You bet. Funny's my middle name." He spikes his hair. "Come on, let's go look at Big Daddy's bookshelf."

Maddie hurries over to the Audubon Book of North American Birds and flips through the pages to the Great White Heron. "This is one of my favorites, Tutor. Isn't he beautiful? Wouldn't you love to ride on his back?"

"Who wouldn't?"

She flips through the pages again. "And look at the Great Horned Owl. I wish I could be as wise as he is and turn my head all the way around to see everything he sees."

Tutor turns his head far to one side, then turns it back real slow, making his eyes big and round. He leans forward and makes a loud shrieking sound, followed by a low quivering, "Who-hooo. Who-hooo."

Maddie lets out a hoot. "I know that's what they sound like, but I've never heard a real owl or seen one in the real world."

"Oh, Maddie, you're missing out on life. Everyone's seen a great horned owl and heard it hoot."

"I want to see one too. Can I, Tutor? Can I?"

"Well, we'll have to see what Big Daddy has to say about that." He glances at his wrist as if there's a watch there, and says, "Whoops. That reminds me. We need to shut this lesson down. I promised I'd be somewhere."

Maddie cries out, "No, Tutor! Don't go."

"I'm afraid I have to, but I'll be back tomorrow, same time, same place, same station. I'll tell you all about Genghis Khan. Well, if we get that far. Anyways, it's been a real pleasure, Little Sister."

He grabs his hat from the coat rack and throws it into the air. It lands perfectly on his head. He gives her a deep bow and disappears out the door.

Maddie's so shocked, she can't move. She didn't say goodbye. What if he doesn't come back tomorrow? What if she never sees him again? What if he's not even real?

She runs out into the living room to catch him, but he's already gone.

She turns away from the door and sees Momma standing by the kitchen with her hands on her hips and a sarcastic look in her eyes. "So?"

"So what?"

"So, what did you two talk about? And what was all that noise? It sounded like a barnyard in there."

Maddie's about to tell her how Tutor pretended to be a chicken, and how he said she might get to see and hear a real owl, and how he taught her about all the different opposites, but the mean look on Momma's face tells her to keep quiet about all that. "We uh...just talked about different things."

"Things?"

"Yes. Just things that I'm supposed to learn so I can think big like Daddy wants me to."

Momma tosses her hair. "Is that right?"

"Yes, Momma. I think Tutor's a really good teacher. I already know so many more things than I did just this morning."

Momma scoffs. "Oh yeah. Like what?"

"Like how some things are bad and other things are wrong, but they're different."

Momma rolls her eyes, then looks scared. "He didn't do anything bad...did he?"

"No, Momma! He's nice!"

Momma doesn't look too sure about that. "Okay. Come have some lunch."

Before Maddie follows her into the kitchen, she runs out on the balcony and looks down to see if she can see Tutor.

Yes! That's him! He looks up and tips his hat just before he disappears beneath the trees. He's real. He really *is*. Maybe he *will* be back tomorrow.

Chapter 5

Maddie can't wait to tell Daddy what she's learned from Tutor, but Momma says he'll be home late tonight. "In fact," she says, "you should go to bed."

"No, Momma. I don't want to."

Momma doesn't care what she wants. She points to the stairs. "Go."

Maddie goes up to her room, but she can't sleep. She's too wound up thinking about how much the world has changed since Tutor came. It happened so fast. When she closes her eyes, she can already feel her head spinning, like he said it would.

She grabs the corner of her white satin quilt and drags it across the shadowy room to the mirror. She sits on the floor, puts her forehead against the cool slick surface of the glass, and whispers, "Oh, Mim, I love Tutor. It's such a miracle he's here. But what if he's not real? Or if he doesn't come back? What will I do?"

Mim touches her fingers through the glass and sighs.

Maddie understands. "You'd love him as much as I do. He does such funny things, like silly wiggles up and down his whole body, and his eyes are so shiny. Sometimes they're blue, sometimes turquoise, and sometimes they're almost black. It's like he's casting a spell over me the whole time."

She pulls the quilt over her lap and touches her finger to Mim's lips. "You can't tell anyone what I'm going to tell you next? Promise?"

Mim nods.

They make their sighing owl oath, and Maddie whispers, "Tutor's my brother."

She waits for Mim to respond, but nothing comes.

"That means he's your brother too, Mim. You should be happy."

She sees worry in Mim's eyes. "I know. I shouldn't have told him about you, but it's okay. We can trust him. He's our brother. We did a blood oath." She takes a deep breath and let's it out quick. "Everything's changed, Mim. I'm not lonely anymore, and I'm not sad." A giggle escapes. "All I am is happy, and kind of scared, and right now I need to go to sleep so I can wake up tomorrow and find out if he's going to be here again. I miss him so much already."

They touch fingertips, and Maddie says, "Goodnight, Mim. Stay close, okay? I might need you."

She curls up on the floor in front of the mirror and pulls the satin quilt up to her chin to keep herself warm while she sleeps. Maybe she'll dream about the house with no doors and the crying baby will be there. Maybe she can find out if he's real.

Instead of dreaming about the house, she wakes up from flying through the night sky on a white horse with Tutor. She opens her eyes and sees Daddy sitting beside her.

"What are you doing on the floor, little Maddie?"

She can't tell him about wanting to be close to Mim. He doesn't know about Mim. "I'm not sure, Daddy. Maybe I was sleep walking."

He gathers her up in the quilt and carries her to bed. He sits beside her and looks at her with curious eyes. "So how was your first day of school with Tutor?"

"Oh, Daddy. I love him so much. He's really nice, and funny, and he said I can see a real Great Horned Owl, if you'll let me."

"An owl, huh?"

"Yes. He said he'd take me, so I can hear it hoot in the real world."

"And where did he say you'd find this owl?"

"I'm not sure. Maybe at the zoo, or some other place where owls live. Can I go? Can I?"

"We'll have to talk to Momma about that."

Maddie sits up quick. "She'll just say no, Daddy. It's not fair that everyone else gets to see a real owl, and I don't."

"We'll see, honey. I'll do my best" He smooths her hair back and smiles. "So tell me, what did you learn today?"

She tries to think how to say it. "Well, I learned about the opposites. You know, up and down, black and white, and good and bad."

"Yes?"

"I mean, Tutor drew a vertical line on the blackboard and put one side of the opposites at the top and the other side at the bottom. Then he showed me how there's a wiggly line over the top of the whole thing, between the extreme ends, and how people can use opposites to influence others by saying certain things are bad, even when they're not, or by claiming that you might go to hell if you do them." She takes a quick breath and rubs her forehead in frustration.

"It's really complicated, Daddy. I mean, I understand it, but it's hard to find all the right words to explain it right now. You know?"

He touches her cheek. "Yes, I think I *do* know. It sounds like he's teaching you some basic ideas that he'll build on later. That's a good approach. Be sure to ask questions, if you need to. Okay?"

"Okay, Daddy. I will." She snuggles under the quilt.

"That's good. Now, go back to sleep. You want to be sharp for your lesson tomorrow." He kisses her forehead and stands up.

"I'll be sharp, Daddy. I promise. Please tell Momma to let me see the owl. If you tell her, she'll have to do it."

"We'll see, Maddie. We'll see."

Chapter 6

The next morning when Tutor arrives, Maddie's so happy to see him she almost gives him a hug, but she knows Momma wouldn't like that. Instead, she presses her arms against the sides of her blue and white flowered dress and smiles. "I'm really glad you came back, Tutor."

"Of course, I came back. Did you think I wouldn't?"

"I wasn't sure. But I'm really glad you did."

Daddy takes them to the study. He closes the door and gives Tutor a curious look. "So, I hear you've got an interesting approach to teaching."

Tutor's eyes shine. "Oh, yes. I've got a bit of magic up my sleeves." He shakes his arms and a stream of gold sparks fly out from the sleeves of his crisp white shirt.

Daddy laughs. "It's good to have diversity in the lessons. We don't want Maddie thinking along one line. She needs a variety of thinking options."

Tutor smiles. "Exactly what I was thinking."

"Okay, then. Go to it. I'm off to work." He shakes Tutor's hand, turns to leave, and turns back. "By the way, I'll work on that field trip to see the owl. I'll let you know."

Tutor nods. "Field trips are good. Very helpful."

When Daddy leaves, Maddie runs to her black leather chair and sits, ready to learn.

Tutor flips his hat to the top rung of the coat rack, tips his head back, and looks down his nose in a snooty way that reminds Maddie of the Mad Hatter. "So, Madam, would you like to start your lesson now, or shall we have tea first?"

Maddie giggles. "I'd like some tea, Mr. Hatter."

"Certainly." Tutor pulls a make-believe cup out of the air and fills it with make-believe tea. He hands it to Maddie and pours himself a cup. "Please. Won't you sit down."

She's already sitting, but she stands and sits back down. She fluffs the skirt of her flowered dress and takes a sip of the tea.

Tutor opens his eyes real wide and shouts, "Why is a raven like a writing desk?"

Maddie's so shocked by his outburst she nearly spits her tea on the floor. She swallows hard and starts coughing. When she recovers, she remembers her line and tilts her head to one side, trying to look like Alice. "Uh...I *think* I can answer that."

Tutor spins the other chair to face her and sits down. "You mean you think you can *find* the answer?"

She throws her hands up with glee. "Exactly!"

He looks down his nose. "Well, why don't you say what you mean?"

She puts her hands on her hips with a snooty look. "At least, *I mean what I say*–that's the same thing as *saying what I mean*, isn't it?"

Tutor rolls his eyes and quivers his head, looking exasperated and quite mad. "It's not the same thing at all! You might just as well say that *I see what I eat* is the same as *I eat what I see* or *I breathe when I sleep* is the same as *I sleep when I breathe*! Pure nonsense."

"I'm sorry." Maddie hangs her head, pretending to be hurt by his words.

"No. No. Don't be sorry, Maddie. I just wanted to show you how a simple rearrangement of words can create a whole new view of things. Do you know why that is?"

His eyes are so black and shiny now, she can't think. "Can you repeat the question, please?"

"Yes. I can. The question is, why are words so powerful? How can changing the order of a few words in a sentence change everything?"

She frowns. "Uh...I'm not sure. Is it because the words have a different meaning depending on what they're next to? I mean...a *cat* is not the same as a *cat in a hat*."

Tutor smiles mischievously. "Exactly." He leans forward with a fake scowl. "But this cat should not be here, he should not be about when your mother is out!"

Maddie shouts, "The Fish."

Tutor touches his finger to his lips. "Shhh. We don't want anyone thinking there's something fishy going on in here. But, yes, the Fish. Do you know him?"

She leans forward and whispers, "Of course, I do. That's Dr. Seuss's fish."

He wags his head in amazement. "Have you read every book ever written?"

"I hope so. How many are there?"

"A lot." He sits up straight and crosses his legs in that tall knee way. He takes a deep breath, holds it, then lets it out slowly. He does it again and again.

Maddie crosses her legs and breathes in and out in the same rhythm.

Tutor lets out a final long breath and smiles. "So, Maddie, yesterday we talked about opposites. Right?"

"Right."

"I'd like to fill in a bit more on that."

"Okay." She lets out a long breath of her own and smiles, feeling relaxed and happy. If she had a real brother, she'd want him to be just like Tutor, but maybe he could be a little brother so she could teach him things. But if he was her little brother, then she wouldn't have a big brother.

She realizes Tutor's waiting for her to come back from her flight of fancy, so she nods and smiles.

He starts his lesson. "Remember, the other day we talked about how innocuous the words *up* and *down* are—"

"Innoculous?"

"*Inno-cu-ous.* Or, innocent. No, that's not right. I mean…well, to use your example of the other day, if the speaker happens to live *up* in a seventh-floor condo and would rather be *down* on the swings, how does that person's longing change the words *up* and *down.*"

"It makes them a lot sadder."

"Yes, it's what you *bring* to the words that matters. The experiences in your life imbue your words and stories with special meaning." His eyes soften and narrow. "Try this, Maddie. Pretend you're reading along in a book, and the words say, *she climbs up the ladder…*You get an image of *her,* whoever she is, in motion, going up a ladder, right?"

"That's right."

"So, where do you think that girl's climbing to, based on your own experience with words and stories?"

Maddie closes her eyes to think. She finds her answer and opens them quick. "I know. She's climbing up to the secret room in the tower to get away from her wicked stepmother." She smirks.

"Okay, so the girl's on a ladder trying to get to the secret room. Then what happens?"

"Uh…Lightning strikes!"

Tutor laughs. "Really? Lightning?"

"Well, it doesn't have to be that."

"No. No. Lightning's good. Let's go there. Okay, so she's balanced on the wobbly ladder, almost up to the door of the secret room, then…lightning strikes."

Maddie throws up her hands and shouts, "Kaboom!"

Tutor touches his lips and looks at the door.

She whispers, "I know. I know. We don't want Momma coming in to spoil things."

Tutor whispers back, "So what happens when lightning strikes."

"The roof catches on fire, and the girl, whose name is Rapunzel by the way, pushes the ladder back from the flames and teeters there, her long golden hair flying in the wind. Then the Prince comes on a flying horse to save her."

"The Prince?"

"Well, maybe he's just a boy she likes, or maybe it's the Blue Fairy. It could be *her*."

Tutor sits back, chuckling. "That's great, Maddie. See what we've done?"

She shakes her head. "No."

"We've taken a word and added another word, and more words, until now we've got a girl named Rapunzel on a tipsy ladder, her long golden hair flying in the wind. It's all just words, but you might really be worried about that girl. I mean, she could be you, since she's got blond hair, and she was created with your words. Maybe you wish we hadn't left her teetering on a tall, rickety ladder. Maybe you wish the lightning hadn't come. But what can you do? It's the world you've created. You put her there, and that's where she is."

He shoots her a sideways look. "Are you with me, Maddie?"

""Yes, I am, Tutor. I see how my words put the girl on the ladder. She was just trying to get up to the secret room, but now she's afraid, afraid she'll be set on fire, or maybe she'll fall. It's what you were saying about the up-and-down opposites, how they're innocent until you connect them with other words, words you already have a feeling about. That's when you see how scary things really are."

Tutor smiles. "You've got the highest-flying mind I've ever encountered, Maddie. How'd that happen in this place where nothing happens?"

"I don't know, Tutor. Maybe it's because I went flying with White Bird, and now I know how to fly."

He nods. "Yes. That's probably it. That sort of thing will definitely give you a new perspective."

She grabs his hand and holds it tight. "Oh, Tutor. I hope we get to see the Great Horned Owl. I'm so sick and tired of seeing the world through books all the time. I need to see the real world for once."

"I'd love to show you that world, Maddie. But we'll have to see if Big Daddy can bring your Momma around. It will be up to him and her."

"It won't work. She'll try to keep me inside. She wants me to be trapped in my condominium cage like White Bird was trapped in his gold cage. But I can't stand it anymore, Tutor. I really can't."

"Patience, Maddie. Patience."

She slaps the arm of her chair. "That's what Daddy always says, but I'm tired of being patient." Tears flow from her eyes and spill down her cheeks. She quickly wipes them away, hoping he didn't see. She doesn't want him to be sad, but he is. She can see it in his eyes.

"I'm sorry, Maddie. I can see it's been hard for you, but it's amazing how well you've survived being caged up here. I'll try to help with getting you some freedom. Okay? We'll keep talking to Big Daddy. See if he can help your Momma not be so scared."

"Okay, Tutor. I hope he can. I need to see that owl."

Chapter 7

Finally, after a long lonely weekend, it's Monday morning. Maddie runs downstairs to Daddy's study and sits in her rolling leather chair waiting for Tutor to arrive. She's so nervous and excited, she can't stop fiddling with the pearl buttons on her white satin blouse. When Daddy finally brings Tutor in and leaves for work, she lets out a long sigh of relief. Tutor's back. He's right in front of her in a silvery white shirt and the slim black pants of his magician suit.

He tosses his hat to the coat rack, gives her a Cheshire Cat smile, and sits in his chair facing her. "So, Maddie, how about we continue our exploration of concepts related to language. You know, the power of the opposites that we talked about before, and how you forever changed the meaning of the words *up* and *down* for me."

She gasps. "Really? I did that?"

"Yes, you gave me a new understanding when you told me about being *up* on the balcony looking *down* at the boys on the swings. There's a deep loneliness in those words now."

"Tutor, I don't remember. Did I tell you about the boys on the swings?"

"Either that, or I saw it in one of those thought bubbles above your head."

She looks over Tutor's head and giggles. "You've got thought bubbles too, you know. They're so big and full of words, they're about to burst."

He hoots and slaps his knee. "You're right about that. My bubbles are always full when I talk to you. So should we learn more about language and how our experience with words affects the way we perceive reality."

"Yes!"

He crosses his knees in that tall way. "Okay, how about this. If a person who only knows Chinese talks to a person who only knows English, will they understand each other?"

"Of course not. But what if one person laughs? The other person might at least know they said something funny."

"Right. Right. That's good. What else?"

"Well, you might know that they said something mean, if they have a mean look on their face."

"Yes?"

"Or, you might know they're saying something silly, if they wiggle all over in a silly way, like you do." She makes her eyes real big and wobbles her head.

He gives her back a whole body wobble that ends with his eyes quivering. "What if two people are speaking the same language, say English, can they be sure they know what the other person is saying?"

"I guess so, if they both know the same words."

"That seems true, doesn't it? And it is true to some degree, but we need to account for each person's unique experience with those words. For example, take your experience with *up* and *down*. I can't truly know what you're saying when you use those two words unless I've been up on the balcony with you, looking down at the boys on the swings."

"That seems right. When you talk, I know most of your words, but I'm not always sure what you're saying."

"That's because I try to use simple words to deliver complex concepts. You *know* the words, but you don't yet know the connections that hold them together as a concept. That's where the real meaning lies. The synapses in your brain are not yet connected in a way that lets you pull in all the bits and pieces you need to understand what I'm saying. But I'll get you there, Maddie. I promise."

"I know you will, Tutor."

His eyes go dark and mysterious while he thinks, then they flash turquoise blue. "The important thing to remember is that the language you learn as you go through life has a direct relationship to the reality you experience. When you add new words, new concepts, metaphors, and knowledge, your language is enriched, and so too is the world you perceive and live in."

Maddie giggles. "I don't know what you just said, but okay."

He holds up his palm. "Here's a question, Maddie. Have you ever spent time reading the dictionary?"

She rolls her eyes. "Why would I do that?"

"You know. To see what's in there."

"I've looked up a lot of words, if that's what you mean. But I haven't read the whole dictionary from front to back."

"That's right. Why would anyone turn to a dictionary at all, except to find the meaning of a particular word? The words are all there, precisely located and defined. They're not going anywhere. But what if you're wearing the lens of a linguist and you want to know when and where a word first emerged in the language, and how it's changed over time? Or what if you look at each word not just to find out what it means, but to think about how it relates to different concepts, or how it's part of a particular hierarchy or categorizing principle." He frowns. "I know. I know. You haven't a clue what I'm saying. Let me work my way into it, then I'll work my way back out and explain what you've missed. Okay?"

She nods. "Okay."

"So, Maddie, let's say we randomly open a dictionary, close our eyes, and move our finger down to a random word. Here, let's do it." He stands up, and she follows him to the giant dictionary on Daddy's black lacquer stand by the window. He lets the dictionary fall open and runs his finger down the page without looking. "Tell me what word is under my finger."

It's a word she doesn't want to think about right now. "Can you pick a different word, Tutor?"

"Why's that?"

"Because it's *mother*, and I don't want to think about her right now."

"Oh, but it's a perfect word for our lesson. The basic definition of the word *mother*, as a noun, is quite simple. That is, a mother is the woman who gave birth to you, or the woman who adopted you. That counts too. Anyways, the word, mother, is easily defined, but the variety of experiences and the number of concepts related to *mother* is huge, once you start thinking about gender and sexuality, the basic structure of the human family, or different animal groups. If you look at the word in biological or physiological terms, or by way of anatomy, you'll be looking at organs and hormones, chromosomes and genes, bones, DNA. makeup, dresses and high-heeled shoes." He giggles and shakes his sleeves, scattering violet sparks across the room. "Did you see what just happened, Maddie?"

"Yes!" she shouts. "I did. You took the word *mother* and scattered it all over the place, like those sparkles from your sleeves."

"Yes. That was fun." He twirls on his heels and comes around to face her. "Do you ever feel like you can read my mind, Maddie?"

She thinks about it. "Not really, but sometimes I feel like I almost know what you're saying. I wait for the next word to see if it will help me understand better, and sometimes it does, but not always." She takes a quick breath. "I'm sorry, that's not very clear, is it?"

"Yes. It *is* clear. That's exactly how I feel when I listen to your lessons."

She gasps. "Really, Tutor? I give you lessons."

"Absolutely. Every time I enter this room and we talk, another part of your world opens up to me. My mind expands as I come to understand your mind and your way of seeing. It's a beautiful thing."

She leans her head against his arm. "I'm so glad you said that, Tutor. I *want* to be a teacher, like you. I want to say something that matters to someone in the world, besides Daddy."

He lifts her chin. "Believe me, Maddie, your words matter to me, and *you* matter to me. More than anything, right now. I never had a sister before."

Their teary eyes meet, and Tutor says, "So, where were we?"

"We were talking about mothers."

"Right. We share that English word. We think we know what we mean when we say it, but we can't know exactly what meaning has been received by the person we're talking to. Their connection to the word may yield different associations and meanings, given their unique experience with their own mother, or perhaps the absence of their mother, or a friend's mother. I mean, when you talk about mothers, you could end up talking about someone turning into a sliver or silver light and disappearing through a crack in the night. That's not in the dictionary."

Maddie wants to ask about the silver light, but he turns and stares out the window with a sad, faraway look in his eyes.

He shakes it off and leads her back to their chairs. "Okay, we know words have a shared meaning that the speakers of a language understand, but beyond that, each of us has a unique meaning for the words based on our experience. Which raises the question: is it important for us to know precisely what another person is saying when they speak?"

"If you really want to understand them."

"So how do we do that if our understanding of the words isn't the same?"

"Well, we could ask questions about what they said."

"What kind of questions, Maddie? And are we still talking about mother?"

"Yes. Mother."

"Okay, what kind of questions do you have about mother?"

"You might want to know if she's a nice mother, or if she's mean."

"Yes, and the next question might be, if she *is* mean, *why* is she mean?"

"I don't know why, Tutor. She just is. But maybe she's not mean. Maybe she's just upset about what Daddy said happened to her, but I don't know what that is." A whimper escapes before she can stop it. "I'm sorry."

"It's okay, Maddie. We can talk about that another time. So what other questions do you have when someone speaks of *mother*?"

"I'd wonder where she is. I mean, your mother. I'd like to meet her."

He sighs. "I'm afraid that's not possible, Maddie."

"Why?"

"Because she's...Like I said, we'll have plenty of time to talk about our mothers later. Okay."

"I understand, Tutor. Should we pick a different word?"

"Yes. This time, you find the word."

They go back to the dictionary by the window. Maddie lets it fall open to a new page. She closes her eyes, moves her finger down the page, and lifts it to show Tutor the word.

He smiles. "Oh yes. Nurture. That's a perfect word."

"What does it mean, Tutor? I think I know, but I'm not sure."

"Yes, it's that kind of word, isn't it? Related to *mother*, by the way. A nurturing mother. The common definition of *nurture* is to care for or encourage the growth and development...of what? A plant? A child? A cat? Of course, there's a huge variety in the type of nurturing we each receive, and that makes for different understandings of what the word, *nurture*, means.

But I'd like to take the word *nurture* into a different conceptual sphere."

"Okay."

"There's an ongoing debate in psychology about whether *nature* or *nurture* has a greater influence on behavior. *Nature,* of course, relates to the physical and genetic characteristics we inherit from our parents, whereas *nurture* relates to environmental influences, our experiences, relationships, and the reinforcement we receive that shapes our behavior."

"Reinforcement? What's that?"

"Think of reinforcement as the rewards and punishments you receive through life that control your behavior. Your Momma might say, 'Good girl,' when you do something she likes. You want to be a good girl, so you keep doing what she likes, and it becomes part of who you are. On the other hand, she might use punishment to control your behavior. She might say, 'you won't be having dinner tonight, if you keep acting that way.' You want dinner, so you act in the way she wants. By the way, if you want to nurture a healthy child, rewards work a lot better than punishment. Punishment can cause harm. It can make the person think they're bad. You and I both have some of that in us, don't we, Maddie?"

"Yes. We do."

"It's interesting. Sometimes a person doesn't care whether they get a reward or punishment, they just want someone to pay attention to them, so they do whatever it takes to get that attention. Think about a puppy. You don't like it barking all the time, so you tell it to stop. If the dog's just looking for attention, and you try to make it stop barking by giving it attention, it's going to bark all the more. You gave it the reward it was looking for."

"I don't have a dog, Tutor, but if I did, what *should* I do to make it stop barking?"

"You should ignore him when he's doing something you don't want him to do and reward him when he's being a good dog. It might help to give him a treat just before you think the barking is about to start, say, when you're almost to the fenced yard where the other dog that he likes to bark at is waiting. Then, if he still barks at the other dog, ignore him. Make him feel like he doesn't exist and eventually he'll stop barking, because he knows you're not going to give him attention."

"Why is it so important to learn that, Tutor? I mean, I don't have a dog."

"It's important because understanding how this works with a dog will help you understand how it works with you, and that will help you understand who you are and how you came to be who you are. It will also help you see how others have come to be who they are. You'll be able to see when you're being rewarded or punished and you can decide your response instead of just reacting.

Be aware, reinforcement doesn't just come from parents. It comes from siblings, teachers, and friends. Rocks, trees, and sunsets. The fairytales we read." He takes a quick breath.

"You mean like *me* and my fairytales?"

"Yes, like you *and* me, Maddie. We've both read a lot of fairytales and other books. You might say books were a fundamental source of our *nurturing*. Interesting, we have that in common. Some people believe we come into this world with a particular self intact, that there's something *innate* about the way we are before our nurturing begins. Others believe we're a tabula rasa, or a blank slate that experience fills in as we encounter the world with our minds and our senses."

She'd like time to think about that, but he keeps talking.

"*Nature* has to do with our DNA, our genes, and the anatomy and physiology that derives from that. Come, let's sit."

They return to their chairs, and he asks, "Do you know anything about genes and DNA?"

She frowns. "Not really."

"Let's see. How do I explain DNA?" He glances at the corners of the ceiling for the answer. "I guess you could say it's that part of Momma and Big Daddy that's in you. The physical part. Or rather, the cellular part. The chromosomes. You know, the DNA and genes that make your body how it is."

He looks doubtful, then his eyes shine as he continues. "DNA makes all humans the same in some ways and different in other ways. It's what differentiates humans from other species: goats, orangutans…spinach."

He toots his make-believe horn and keeps going. "Within DNA, unique genes make you physically unique, I mean. Genetically. Oh, Maddie, there's so much to learn. It's hard to think conceptually about genetics without knowing all the facts and details. Sometimes, you have to learn all that before you can go with the flow of the concept, which is what I like to do."

"I think I get some of what you're saying about the DNAs and stuff. Is it like when Daddy says my nose is adorable like Momma's, or Momma says I'm lean as a bean like Daddy?"

"Yes. Yes, Maddie. That's it. That's DNA."

"Do I have any unique parts that are just me?"

"There's no question, the unique part of you is your mind. The key is to keep feeding it knowledge, and not cling to any one way of thinking about things. Be a generalist rather than a specialist. Perceive from the vantage point of the inbetween worlds, that we talked about before. A specialist learns all the concepts and details related to a particular subject at a deep level. They become experts in their field, but that can result in a narrow view. I'd rather to be a generalist and fly between worlds."

"I want that too."

"I know, Maddie. We've established that, and fly we will." He glances at his wrist. "Okay. First thing tomorrow, we'll get back to that."

Maddie shouts, "No, Tutor. Don't leave."

"'Fraid I have to, Little Sister. But don't worry. I'll always be back. I promise."

"You better. It would hurt too much if I lost you."

"Same here, Maddie. Same here."

Chapter 8

Daddy's off in Japan, and Momma's already in the bathtub, drowning herself in whiskey. Today, that's okay with Maddie. Tutor's coming. She puts on her purple and pink unicorn dress, slips her feet into her white satin ballet slippers, and runs downstairs to practice her pirouettes in the living room while she waits for Tutor to arrive. She's never felt so free to be herself.

It gets later and later. She starts to worry that he's not coming, but then the doorbell chimes. She opens the door and there's Tutor with a blue box in his arms.

She gasps. "Oh boy. Is that a present for me?"

He smiles. "Sure, we can call it that, if you like. Can I come in?"

"Of course, you can." She pulls him straight to Daddy's study, closes the door, locks it, then turns to explain. "We've got to be really quiet today. Daddy's on a long business trip to Japan, which means Momma might try to come in and keep us from doing what we want to do."

"Okay. We'll keep things down." He sets his box on Daddy's desk. "So, do you want to see what we've got here?"

"Yes, please." She goes to his side.

When he lifts the lid, she can hardly believe her eyes. The box is filled with sunglasses. Red and blue ones, yellow and green, pink, heart shapes and stars, some with diamond frames. "They're beautiful, Tutor. What are they for?"

"Think of them as conceptual lenses." He leans against the desk with his legs crossed at the ankles like Daddy does sometimes. They both have that shiny black hair, blue eyes, mischievous smiles, though, lately, Daddy hasn't shown his much. Did he ever?

Tutor's lips twitch, like he's trying to hide a smile. "That's what I love about you, Maddie. You're always slipping off on your own train of thought."

"I'm sorry, Tutor. I didn't mean to."

"Don't be sorry. It's a good thing. It lets me know you're thinking, and it always leads me right back to what I was saying."

"What *were* you saying?"

"I was saying there's a tendency to think we all perceive reality in the same way. But that's not true. We may have the same sensory organs, and our brains function more or less the same, but our minds, where perception takes place, are unique because they're constructions of our life experience. Each of us arrived in the stream of life at a unique time and place, and therefore, our experience, and thus our minds and perception of reality, are unique as well."

"Of course, there are some things we all agree to agree on. For example, all humans know they are human and recognize other humans as human. That's basic. But language and culture make us different. Like we talked about before, the words and concepts we use to describe and interpret the world around us determine what we see, how we understand what we see, what we hear and feel, what we love and hate."

"Language is powerful. We can think about things that aren't there, things that happened in the past, or even in the future, if we're creative or good at extrapolation. We can communicate complex ideas to each other, even if our language isn't exactly the same. We all have words for color, blue, black, brown. Even if we don't see those colors exactly the same, we can speak about them. Concepts, some simple, some complex, help us communicate across the gulf of our differences."

Maddie looks at Tutor and shakes her head. She's been trying to keep up, but it's hard to do because of all the different things he throws in. How's she supposed to remember it all?

He pulls at his lips and then frowns. "The main thing to remember, Maddie, is that language is powerful. It creates the lens you see through when you look at the world around you. The more you know about that lens, the more you'll understand yourself, and the more you'll understand others. That's key."

"What kind of a lens do I have, Tutor? Do you know?"

"Anyone might assume your perspective is narrow after spending your life inside this condo. But all the books you've read have given you a remarkably expansive view. Your lens is like a prism, offering countless ways to see the world." He nods toward his box. "These conceptual glasses will help us explore that idea."

He digs through the box and pulls out a pair of lime-green sunglasses with fiery red-orange lenses. Slipping them on, he hands her a violet pair with sparkling blue heart-shaped glass and a diamond-studded frame.

She slips on her glasses and looks around. "It's funny in here, Tutor. From the outside, the glass sparkles with light, but inside, it's dark. I can hardly see."

"Your pupils need to accommodate to the new level of light, just as our minds will need to accommodate to a new level of understanding once we start looking at the world through the different lenses. Come." He leads her to the leather chairs and they sit down. "Okay. Let's see how this works. My glasses are green with red-orange glass. So, what kind of a world do you think I see?"

Maddie takes her glasses off and looks him over. "I'm not sure what you see, but you look a lot like a red-eyed tree frog."

He sputters a laugh. "A red-eyed tree frog, you say? Okay, how does a red-eyed tree frog see the world?" He arches his eyebrows over the top of his glasses and gives her a wide frog grin below.

"Well," she says in her know-it-all voice, "Daddy's Audubon book says they have big bulging eyes on the sides of their heads so they can see what's ahead *and* behind."

Tutor takes a floppy hand pose. "My dear, are you saying I can see myself coming *and* going?"

She giggles. "Yes, you're just like Doctor Doolittle's Pushmi–Pullyu, only it has two heads, and you don't."

He throws back his head and lets out a loud squawk. "Lord save us! How does it make up its mind?"

Maddie hoots. "That's what the duck says to Doctor Doolittle. Have you read every book ever written, Tutor?" She smirks, remembering how he asked *her* that question.

He sniggers. "I don't know. How many books are there?"

"A lot."

He looks over his glasses and gives her that wide-eyed tree frog grin again. "So, my young herpetologist, what else do you know about Agalychnis callidryas?"

She holds up a pretend microphone and puts on her TV announcer's voice. "Agalychnis callidryas, more commonly known as red-eyed tree frogs, are well-known for seeing things at night when others can't see anything. They have really delicate skin and don't like to be touched, because they can absorb stuff from your hands, like lotion, that might make them sick."

Tutor borrows her microphone. "That's right, my dear, and they can climb trees. Am I right? Or am I right? By the way, I suppose you know that the Pushmi-Pullyu is related to the Abyssinian Gazelles and the Asiatic Chamois—on its mother's side, and that its father's great–grandfather was the last of the Unicorns. By the way, did you know we were going to talk about Unicorns when you wore that dress?"

She pokes at a pink unicorn and smiles. "No, I *didn't* know, but I did know they climb trees!" She shouts, "After all, they *are* tree frogs! They're lime-green with blue trim around the edges and bright red-orange eyes, the same color as their suction-cup toes. It's because of those toes that they're good at climbing trees."

Tutor jumps out of his chair and pretends to climb a tree with sticky suction-cup toes. Maddie joins the fun. When they get to the top of their trees, they fall to the floor, croaking and hopping around like red-eyed tree frogs.

Tutor rolls onto his back, gasping for air. He recovers and sits up, cross-legged. "That's a good start with the glasses, Maddie. But what about your purple heart lenses, or should I say, *violet*, with sparkly blue glass? How do *they* help you see?"

She puts them back on and looks around the room. Her view through the glass gives her a dark, sad feeling, like she felt before Tutor came into her world. She doesn't want to feel like that. She pulls the glasses off and sees herself smiling in the sparkly mirrored side of the glass, but she doesn't know what it means or how to explain it to Tutor.

He rolls onto his side and lifts his tree-frog glasses. "So. What do you see?"

She shrugs. "I guess it depends on whether I'm inside the glass seeing a dark sad world, or outside seeing a bright sparkly world where I'm happy."

"That last one! It's perfect for our lesson."

"Okay."

"So, I'm the frog with extraordinary red eyes, and you're the reflective side of the mirrored lens. What do we both see?"

She gasps. "I know. If I'm the reflection in the mirror and if you're a frog looking in the mirror, then I'm a frog too, and that's how we both see the world. Right?"

Tutor looks stunned. "Maddie. Maddie. Maddie. You never cease to amaze me. I'm on the verge of teaching you a new concept and you take a quantum leap right over my head. You've already arrived where I was looking to take us."

She blinks. "I have?"

"Absolutely."

"Okay, but I'm not even sure what that means."

He rolls onto his knees and does a little frog hop. "Well, looking at it from my point of view, as a red-eyed tree frog, I, like most people looking at someone else, see mostly a reflection of myself. It's called projection. We project all kinds of things onto other people. Our hopes and dreams, our desires, our hate, our love. Sometimes, we even project what we dislike most about ourselves."

Maddie thinks about that. "You mean, Momma's not really mean? It's me being mean?"

"Not necessarily. I don't mean to say we can't see anything about the world that *isn't* a projection. It's just that we need to understand how our minds work. That way, we can get some distance from our subjectivity and get closer to the real truth of things, or at least reach a broader understanding where we can see from more than one perspective. You know?"

"Not really."

"What I mean is, I want you to be free, Maddie. Free from your past. Free from your experience and indoctrination. Free to fly on the wings of possibility without experiential and cultural inhibitions, unless you choose to use them as a guide for seeing and stabilizing yourself, if you ever need that."

"You mean I can be free like White Bird?"

"Exactly."

"But how can I be free if Momma won't let me do anything. I can't even go out on the balcony anymore. After I flew with White Bird, she made Gardener put a lock on the sliding window."

A glimmer of sadness crosses Tutor's eyes. "I guess, until your Momma finds her way back from whatever's hurting her, we'll have to find our freedom here in Daddy's study. We'll use our minds and the conceptual glasses to explore the world beyond. We'll look through the lens of psychology and biology, architecture and art. We can even put ourselves in the mind of the Mongolian mongrel, Genghis Khan, if you like. But not now. Today, let's stick to exploring the world of frogs and mirrors and how they each create a particular view of the world."

He jumps up and finds another pair of green glasses with red lenses like his and gives them to her. "Come. Let's explore a bit more about being frogs."

They go to the window and look out through their glasses. Maddie gets caught up in the contrasts. "Look how dark blue the sky is, Tutor. And how completely white the clouds are. It's beautiful. I wish we were out there flying with White Bird."

He smiles. "Yes, wouldn't that be grand. Maybe some-day we *will* find your White Bird. 'Til then, let's be satisfied with being here. Okay?"

"Okay."

He drops back to the floor, squats like a frog, and puts his head forward, tipping it both ways. He flicks out his tongue and takes a big swallow.

Maddie groans. "Oh, ick, did you just eat a fly?"

"No. No. That was another red-eyed tree frog I ate. Didn'tcha know? Us tree frogs are car...nivorous. Canni-bals, I guess you'd say." He stretches his mouth out in a ferocious frog grin.

"Yuck," she says. "That's a double ick." She plops down on all fours, takes a little frog leap, croaks, and falls onto her side, laughing.

Tutor runs through a series of silly frog faces, until they're both rolling on their backs, holding their stomachs.

"Wait, Tutor. What's that." Maddie stares at the door with wide-opened eyes to tell him there's someone there. It's got to be Momma.

She puts her finger over her lips, gets up, and tiptoes to the door. She puts her ear against the wood. She can't hear a thing, but she's sure Momma's out there.

The doorknob turns. Maddie presses the full weight of her body against the door to keep her out, but Momma pushes hard and sends her sprawling across the floor. She storms into the study looking like a bird in her black-and -gold Chinese Empress robe. Squawking, she flaps her black wings. "What the hell's going on in here? What's he been doing to you, Maddie?"

Maddie crawls over to protect Tutor, but he doesn't need it. He gets to his feet, grabs her hand, and quickly pulls her to her feet. He takes off his glasses and takes a step toward Momma. "I'm glad to see you, Missus. The Boss said you might drop in."

Momma glares at him. "Don't be a smart ass."

"I'm serious. I'm glad you're here. We were talking about something that might be of interest to you."

Momma steps back, looking suspicious. "Like what?"

"We were talking about how the times we're born in and the experiences we have during our life make us unique in all the world. And how that uniqueness brings us to perceive the world in a particular way. Do you ever think about that?"

Momma flaps her black wings higher. "What the—? Get out of here. Now. You hear me?"

Maddie jumps between them, pushing Momma back as she screams, "No Momma! No! He didn't do anything. We were just learning how tree frogs think and how they see the world. I promise. That's all it was."

"Frogs?" Momma yells. "*Frogs?*"

Maddie grabs Momma's black wings and pulls her away from Tutor. "Yes, Momma. We were just pretending to be tree frogs so we could learn how they think and how they see the world. It was just one of my lessons. It's what Daddy wants me to learn."

Momma gives her a vicious look and shakes free of her grip. "Daddy. Daddy. I'm sick of hearing what Daddy wants." She grips Tutor's arm and pulls him out of the study and all the way to the front door.

Maddie stays right behind, trying to pull Momma back, but she's too strong.

When they get to the door, Tutor gently unwinds Momma's hand from his wrist. "It's okay, Missus. I'll go, peacefully. But I sure do hope you'll see your way to letting me come back."

Momma gives him the meanest look Maddie's ever seen. "That's not going to happen. We don't need you here stirring things up." She pushes him out the door and slams it so hard the chandeliers chime.

Maddie can't believe what Momma's done. She's ruined everything. "No, Momma. Please! Don't make Tutor go. What will I do without Tutor?"

Chapter 9

Maddie glares at Momma and races to the sliding glass window. She twists and yanks at the lock, but it won't budge. Desperate to see Tutor one last time, she presses her face against the glass, straining to see him below.

There he is. On the sidewalk.

He looks up and tips his hat just before he disappears beneath the trees.

She turns from the window with a sadness in her heart that's so huge she can hardly breathe. If she'd never known Tutor, it wouldn't hurt so much. But she *did* know him. He's her friend, her teacher, and the brother she's never had. She needs Daddy so bad right now. He'll get Tutor back. He just has to.

Momma stands in the kitchen doorway, hands on her hips with a look that says she doesn't care how much it hurts. "What's the big deal, Maddie. He's just some smart aleck boy Daddy brought here to confuse you. I say, good riddance."

Maddie slaps the window. "That's not true. He's not a smart aleck. He's just smart. He knows everything about everything. He understands all the opposites and how to use sunglasses to help people see the world in different ways. Nobody else knows that."

Momma scoffs. "That's not smart. That's wacky. Don't you get it? He's filled your head with a bunch of nonsense for his own amusement. I'm afraid it's going to take some drastic measures to get you straightened out."

Maddie knows what that means; Momma's threatened her before. "No, Momma. No! I can't live in Littletown. I'll die, if you take me there. I'll never learn anything about anything, except…chickens."

"Don't knock it. You can learn a lot from chickens."

Maddie wails. "Why, Momma? Why did you send him away?"

"I did it for you, Maddie. Believe me, I've done you a favor. You'll thank me someday."

"No! I'll never thank you. And I'll never forgive you. You're mean, Momma. All you ever think about is yourself. You can go live in Littletown, if you want to, but I won't go!"

Momma steps closer, poking her finger in the air like a knife. "You'll go, where I tell you to go. I'm your mother. Remember?"

"You just want to put me in a Littletown cage. But I'm not going. I'm staying here with Daddy. When he gets home, he'll bring Tutor back. I know he will."

Momma rubs her forehead like it hurts. "Damn it! I'm in a cage too. I'm just like that bird you set free. Trapped." She glares at the floor, then looks at Maddie with scared eyes. "I need to go back to Littletown, Maddie. I just have to."

The frantic look in her eyes worries Maddie, but she can't have her way this time. "I won't go, Momma. You'll have to go by yourself." She hits her chest with her fist, trying to break up the hard ball of pain and guilt that's building there.

Momma turns away. She takes a few steps into the kitchen, then turns back. "Believe me, Maddie, you and I will do just fine without that boy."

"That's not true! *What* will we do? *Nothing*? Like we did before Tutor came? You'll stay in the bathtub or your bedroom with your whiskey and the only thing I'll have to do is read books." She stomps the floor. "I've read all the books. I've watched all the movies, and listened to all the songs. I'm tired of learning that way. I need to see the *real* world. Please, Momma, please. Let me see the world."

Tears roll down her face, off her chin, and onto her dress, darkening a pink unicorn. She tries to focus on that, but she can't stop thinking about Tutor and how much she's going to miss him.

Momma comes over and lifts her chin with a hint of softness in her eyes, but she doesn't say she's sorry. She turns away and shuffles around the room, muttering nonsense words. She stops in the corner and shakes her head, real hard, like she's trying to shake away a bad thought. Or maybe she's trying to shake sparkles out of her ears, like Tutor. No. Momma doesn't have any sparkles, and she doesn't have any funny faces or funny voices, or important things to teach. She only knows how to look mean, or sad, or like somebody's hurt her feelings. All looks that make Maddie feel like she's to blame for everything bad.

Momma comes back from the corner with an uncertain look that might mean she's sorry for what she's done. "You don't understand, Maddie. I've got a hurt inside me that's so big it will never heal. I need to go home where I feel safe."

"I know that, Momma, but what about me and how I feel?"

Momma doesn't care about that. She frowns and heads upstairs to her whiskey like she always does when she's too sad, or too hurt, or too scared to do anything else.

Now, Maddie's alone with a trapped feeling that makes her want to crash the window out with a chair so she can fly away. But where would she fly? She doesn't know where Tutor lives, so how could she find him? And, besides, it would hurt Daddy so much if he came home and found out she'd left the same way as White Bird.

She glances around the living room at the hard white walls. The cold white leather couch. The black leather chairs. The coffee table gleams with it's slick glass top and sharp chrome edges. A glint of sunlight on White Bird's gold cage catches her eye, drawing her near. The cage looks so empty, it's like White Bird was never there. She can't stand to look at it.

She runs to the study, closes the door, and leans back against the cold hard wood, trying not to cry. She sees Tutor's box of sunglasses on the desk and realizes she needs to hide those from Momma. But where?

The coat closet might be a good place. Momma never goes out, so she never needs a coat. She'll never look there.

She carries the box out to the closet, and crawls in far enough to push the box behind the longest raincoats in the back. She sits in the dark beneath the coats, trying not to cry.

Finally, she crawls out and goes back to the study to figure out what to do. That's when she sees Tutor's hat on the coat rack and realizes he didn't tip his hat to her down on the sidewalk. She made the whole thing up.

It's hopeless. She's never going to see Tutor again. She's right back in the same sad, lonely world she lived in before. Without White Bird. Without Tutor. Without anyone, except Momma. She won't even have Daddy to talk to until he gets home.

She grabs Tutor's hat and lies on the flying horse rug with Tutor's hat over her face. She stares up into the darkness, breathing in the sweet scent of his hair, remembering his turquoise blue eyes. Will she ever see them sparkle again?

She needs Daddy.

Maybe he's already on a plane flying home across the Pacific Ocean. She grabs the thick mane of the flying horse, closes her eyes, and there she is, outside Daddy's little round window on the plane. He sees her and blows her a kiss, mouthing the words. "I'm almost home, Maddie. I'm almost there. Don't worry. I'll get Tutor back. I promise."

She hopes that's true.

Chapter 10

Another sad day and Maddie's back on the floor in the study staring into the blackness of Tutor's hat with her hand on the mane of the flying white horse. She calls on every bit of magic she knows, but she still can't see Tutor's face. All she gets is a glimpse of his blue eyes and the black shine of his hair when it's spiked up. She can't see his smile. She can't hear his silly giggle, like when they were acting like red-eyed tree frogs. Will she ever have a friend like Tutor again? Will she have another friend at all? Or will Momma keep her locked up the rest of her life like a bird in a really small cage. She can't live like that. She has to be free.

She scrambles to her feet, runs to the study window, unlocks it, and pushes up the wood frame. It doesn't go up very far, but maybe she can squeeze through if she takes out the screen. She pushes around the edges of the screen until it lets loose and falls. Now, if only she had that ladder from that story she made up with Tutor, she could climb down to the playground. She wouldn't care if the wind blew hard or if lightning struck and set her hair on fire. She'd climb down and find Tutor, no matter how hard it was.

She squeezes her head and shoulders through the narrow opening and looks down. There's a ledge she could reach if she had that ladder, but she doesn't have it. What else? The metal trellis that holds the climbing wisteria

might be strong enough to hold her, if she goes slow. But
what if it doesn't hold her? What if she falls? It's a long way
down and the landing doesn't look as soft as last time. She
wishes White Bird was there to help her fly.

She hears a sound behind her and looks back. Daddy's
standing there with his hands on his hips and big question
marks in his eyes.

"Uh...What are you doing here, Daddy? I...didn't know
you were home."

"The question *is*, what are you doing, Maddie?"

"Uh, nothing. I was just trying to, uh...see if White
Bird came back. I mean, I thought I saw him."

"Is that right?" He comes over to the window and
looks out. "You weren't thinking of climbing out there,
were you?"

"No, Daddy. There's nothing to climb on. I'd fall."

"Yes. You *would* fall." His eyes narrow. "What happened to the screen?"

"Uh...I was trying to get it out, so I could...uh...see
White Bird better. That's when it accidentally fell. I'm really
sorry." She whimpers, "Please, Daddy, please. You have to
get Tutor back."

He looks surprised. "What do you mean, get him
back? Where did he go?"

"Momma sent him away because we were pretending
to be red-eyed tree frogs. You know, so we could see the
world like they do. Momma came in, with her own key,
and said we were doing something bad, but we weren't,
Daddy. I promise. We were just laughing and rolling on the
floor because it was so funny to be tree frogs, you know,
leaping around, climbing trees, catching flies and stuff."

Daddy leans against the wall with his arms folded and his ankles crossed, like Tutor does sometimes. "Tell me what happened, Maddie. What did she do?"

"The door was locked, but she came in anyway. She was really mad, and she told Tutor to leave. It didn't matter what we said, she pulled him all the way to the front door and pushed him out. She slammed the door so hard, it made the chandeliers ring. Please, Daddy. Tell her it's not fair. She has to let Tutor come back."

Daddy picks her up and sits her on the edge of his desk, which makes her feel small, when she needs to feel big. He looks so deep into her eyes she can't look away. "Now, listen, Maddie. You tell me honestly, what were you doing at the window? I mean it. It's important for you to tell me the truth."

A hard ball of pain pushes up into her throat and bursts out as a long lonely wail she can't stop.

Daddy holds her and rubs her back like she's a little girl again. "It's okay, Maddie. It's alright. I'm here."

She can't stop crying. "I was scared, Daddy. I didn't think I'd ever see Tutor again. I thought I'd live the rest of my life stuck in this condo cage with no friends, or anything. I can't do it anymore, Daddy. It hurts too much."

He holds her tighter. "So, you were trying to get out?"

She buries her face in his chest. "I didn't know what else to do, Daddy."

He gently pushes her back and looks deep into her eyes again. "You're not a bird, Maddie. You can't fly. You've got to stop trying."

"Birds are free, Daddy. They can go wherever they want to. I can't go anywhere or do anything. And now, Momma won't let Tutor come to teach me. Even the balcony is locked, so I can't watch the kids in the playground. I'm too lonely, Daddy. I'm way too lonely."

He touches her cheek with the edge of his finger. "I know you are, honey. I'll talk to her. We'll work it out. I promise."

"Thank you, Daddy. Thank you. I knew you'd help."

Chapter 11

Maddie can't sleep. She's too wound up trying to believe in the possibility of impossible things. Tutor's coming to talk to Momma and Daddy this morning. They're going to decide if he can come back to teach her.

She crosses her fingers, her legs, and her toes, wishing on all her lucky numbers and stars that Daddy will be the one to decide. If Momma decides, the answer will be no.

Why does Momma hate Tutor so much? They weren't doing anything bad. Just laughing at how silly tree frogs are. She told Daddy that, but what if he didn't believe her? What if he believes Momma's side of the story?

She tries counting sheep, but it doesn't help. It's going to be a long wait for morning.

Finally, after what seems like a million years, light streams through the gap in the curtain, telling her it's time to get up. She strips off her nightgown and puts on a white cotton blouse and the lucky four-leaf clover skirt she set out last night.

She waves to Mim and races downstairs where she sits on the sofa, with her eyes closed, willing the doorbell to chime.

It doesn't chime, but she can hear Momma and Daddy arguing in the kitchen about something. That's not good. If she can't make them stop, things could go bad when Tutor arrives.

She bursts into the kitchen with a sunny smile, twirls around the room, and stops next to the table. "Good morning, Momma. Good morning, Daddy. Did you both sleep tight?"

Daddy chuckles. "Yes, quite tight. How about you?"

She rolls her eyes to the ceiling in an exaggerated way. "I couldn't sleep at all."

Momma lifts the blond curls off her neck and lets them fall back down around her shoulders. She shoots Maddie a little smile. "I'm sorry you couldn't sleep, honey. But that's alright. You don't need to be here. You should go back to bed."

"No, Momma! I can't go to bed. Tutor's coming!" She looks at Daddy for help.

His eyes tell her to sit down.

He looks at Momma and tips his head toward the stove. "Why don't you get her something to eat?"

Momma scowls and goes to the stove. She puts something from the frying pan onto a plate, turns, and clunks it down on the glass table in front of Maddie. "Eat," she says, "then go to your room."

Maddie sticks her fork into the scrambled eggs just as the doorbell chimes.

She jumps up to answer it, but Daddy says, "No, Maddie. Stay here. Momma and I need to talk to Tutor alone."

"No, Daddy, please. I need to talk too."

"I'm sorry, Maddie. You stay here and finish your breakfast, then go upstairs. We'll talk later. I promise."

He heads out of the kitchen to answer the door.

Momma tries to block Maddie at the kitchen door, but she ducks under her arm and catches up. "Please, Daddy, please! Don't leave me out."

His eyes say, don't worry, honey, everything will be fine. When he opens the door, Maddie gasps. Tutor's so serious, and he's not wearing his magician suit, his Mad Hatter hat, or his sparkly red shoes. He's wearing a regular short-sleeve shirt with plain tan pants. He could easily be someone else. "Tutor? Is that you?"

"It's nice to see you too, Maddie." His voice is friendly, but he keeps his head down so she can't see if his eyes are bright turquoise, regular blue, or maybe black to go with how serious he is.

He tips his hat to Daddy and holds out his hand. "Hello, Boss. Good to see you again."

Daddy grabs his hand and shakes it. "It's good to see you too, Tutor."

Momma comes out of the kitchen.

Tutor steps forward offering his hand, but Momma won't take it. She pulls back, scowling.

Daddy shoots Maddie an *I'm sorry* look. Then he touches Momma's shoulder and Tutor's elbow and says, "Come, you two. Let's go talk."

Maddie wants to yell, "Let me talk too!" Instead, she clamps her hand over her mouth and stays by the front door, watching them go. Just before Tutor enters the study, he looks back with a dazzling smile and bright turquoise eyes. He shakes his sleeves, scattering sparks of gold that rise and fly around the room like honey bees gathering pollen in the morning light. "Oh, Tutor," she whispers. "It really is you. You're back. How did you know I love bees?"

He gives her a secret smile and disappears behind the door.

She twirls around the room, gathering bees and putting them in the pockets of her four-leaf clover skirt. She stops by the balcony window and swirls her skirt, making the bees buzz. It's so easy to believe in magic when Tutor's here. So easy to believe in impossible things. The most impossible thing she needs right now is for Momma to say, "Yes, Tutor can teach her."

She presses her ear against the study door, but she can't hear a thing. Maybe they're not talking. That would be bad.

She really needs to hear what's going on. But how?

"She thinks of something that might work. She runs to the kitchen, grabs a glass, and takes it to the coat closet. Crawling over the boots and shoes beneath the coats, she reaches the very back. She can almost see Daddy sitting on his side of the desk with Momma and Tutor on the other side in the black leather chairs with wheels.

When she puts the small end of the glass against the wall and presses her ear against the wide open end, it works, just like she knew it would. She can hear them perfectly.

Momma squawks, "Don't give me that. I know what you've been doing. You've been filling her head with nonsense, telling her ridiculous stories about everything under the sun, including me. I won't let you turn her against me. I won't."

"That's not true," Daddy says. "He's not doing any of that. Tutor's trying to help our Maddie, and you too. You've kept our girl locked up for too long. She's not going to stay here forever. Don't you see it? She's bored. Tutor can keep her occupied a bit longer, but you need to prepare yourself for letting her go out into the world. She needs to experience life for herself. She needs friends. She needs access to knowledge and opportunity so she can decide what to do with her life. Don't you want that for her, honey?"

Momma whimpers, "No. I can't lose her too. I can't. You know, I can't."

Maddie can't understand why she's talking about losing someone again. Who did she lose?

Daddy's voice comes through the wall, low and reassuring. "You're not going to lose her, but we have to do something. Our Maddie's lonely. That's why she followed the bird off the balcony. She was trying to fly out of here. It's dangerous for her to be thinking like that all the time. Tutor can help her fly *safely*, with her mind, right here in the study. Am I right, Tutor?"

"Yes, Boss. I can do that. We can fly a good distance on what she already knows and what she wants to know, and while we're flying with ideas, I can help her prepare for living in the real world. I can help her sort through all that knowledge and help her structure it in a way that allows her to make sense of it, on her own terms. I can help her understand the world by way of different concepts; psychology and philosophy. History, and war."

"War?" Momma howls. "Why war? That's the ugly side of things. I don't want her learning about war, or violence, or people taking things that don't belong to them."

Maddie whispers, "Listen to Tutor, Momma. He knows what I need to know, and he knows I need to be free to do things outside."

Tutor's voice comes back low and gentle like Daddy's. "You're right, Missus. War is the ugly side of things, but it might be good for her to have some knowledge of it. A lot of war goes on in the world at different levels. I can give her tools to help her understand why wars arise, how they grow from the way we live, from our psychology, our biology, and our greed."

Momma scoffs. "What does a boy like you know about war?"

"Quite a bit, actually." There's silence for a minute, then Tutor continues, "I'll tell you a story. When I was a boy, I lost my father to war, then I lost my mother to grief. I was young, but I wanted to understand what happened to them and why it happened, so I studied war. I studied the history of wars around the world through time. I learned about the power of patriotism and how revenge is used strategically to build the level of animosity needed to turn young men into killers, even though they've been taught their whole lives that it's wrong to kill. There are a lot of complex concepts involved in war. Knowing how it works will help Maddie understand war as well as propaganda of all kinds. It will help her see things with a wise and measured mind. Like the Boss says, some day, she'll be out in the world on her own. It will be good if she can think for herself and not be drawn in by propaganda."

"What?" Momma yells. "You want to try that out on Maddie? You want to twist her mind all around like yours? I won't let that happen!"

There's silence behind the wall, then she hears Daddy clear his throat. She can almost see him lean forward, an elbow on the desk, his chin in his hand, a serious look in his eyes. He says, "I think we need to try this again, Momma. Let Tutor do what he knows how to do. I know you're afraid. I understand that, but our girl needs all the knowledge she can hold. You're afraid for her to go to a regular school, so you're going to have to buck up and let her learn here, with Tutor."

"Sure. I'll buck up. Sure. Why not? What do I have to say about any of it anyway? I'm losing my girl. There's nothing I can do to stop it." Her voice trails off into a sad whimper.

Maddie hears the fear and sadness in Momma's voice, and there's anger too. But she said she'd do what Daddy said. Can she be trusted? Hopefully, this time, she can. Maybe, for once, the impossible thing *will* happen.

Chapter 12

Tutor comes back the next day. They go to Daddy's study and sit in the black leather chairs. Maddie follows his gaze around the room until their eyes land on Daddy's stained-glass lamp. The colors of the fruit are glowing bright, as if nothing bad happened. But it did, and now, even though she's wearing her lucky four-leaf clover skirt for the second day, she's still afraid of what Momma might do next time Daddy goes on one of his long business trips to Japan.

She grabs Tutor's hand and holds it to her chest. "What if Momma changes her mind? What if she decides you can't teach me?"

He takes a deep breath then lets it out long and slow. "Well, I guess Big Daddy will either set it right, or he won't. In the meantime, we have work to do. Right?"

"Right." She agrees but she's still worried.

Tutor turns his chair to face her. He smiles and shines his turquoise eyes as he spikes up his hair and pulls on his little beard. When he tips his head back, blue sparks fly around the room, telling her the magic is still there.

"So, Maddie. Should we pick up where we left off?"

"Yes!" She looks at the floor trying to remember where they left off and sees something that distracts her. "What happened to your Dorothy shoes, Tutor?"

"Oh. You noticed that, did you?"

"Of course, I did. Those shiny black ones are nice, but they don't sparkle like your red Dorothy shoes."

He gives her a teasing look. "Well, turns out those shoes had a mind of their own. Took off in the middle of the night and went to the Prince's ball. Cinderella, you know. Guess they thought they were glass slippers."

Maddie giggles and claps her hands. "Oh, good. You're just as silly as you were before"

He shakes his head. "No, Maddie. Not quite as silly. We've got a lot to cover. We better take a more serious approach."

"Oh no. Does that mean we can't laugh?"

"Of course not. We'll laugh our heads off, from time to time." He waggles his head like it's about to fall off.

She wants to giggle, but holds back. "Okay. Let's be serious."

Tutor stands and wiggles his finger for her to follow him. "I want to show you something."

They go to the window and look out at the cloud animals flying across the sky above the tall buildings. She feels the warmth of his arm against hers and knows he's really back. And, yes, he's her tutor, but he's also her friend and her blood brother.

He nudges her arm. "So, Maddie, tell me, have you ever been outside this condo? Out there with the clouds, and the trees, the buildings, and those little people down on the sidewalk."

She sees it all and says, "No."

"Never?"

"Well, I told you about flying with White Bird, and there was that one other time in Littletown."

"That's right. Littletown. When was that?"

"I'm not sure. Maybe four years ago, or a little more. We went there to watch Granny die."

"That's right. You told me she died. Would that be Momma's momma, or Daddy's momma?"

"Momma's."

"That experience must have had a huge influence on you."

"I think it did."

"It's good to look back at that kind of powerful experience to see what it taught you and how it has influenced you over time. Do you want to do that?"

Maddie's not sure she wants to think about Granny dying, but it's Tutor asking, so she has to say yes. She gives him a nod. "Okay."

They go back to their chairs.

Tutor looks deep in her eyes, like Daddy does when he wants her to focus on what he's about to say. "Okay, Maddie. Relax your shoulders, close your eyes, and breathe in. Hold it, and breathe out. Breathe in. Breathe out. Long, slow breaths. Now, take yourself back to that time in Littletown. See what comes to mind."

She tries to see it, but there's nothing there.

He touches her arm. "Anything at all, Maddie. Tell it like a story from one of your books."

She takes another deep breath, lets it out slowly, and the story begins. "Once upon a time, we were staying at Granny's house, where Momma lived before Daddy came and swept her off her feet and took her to the city to live with him."

"Is that how it went?"

"That's what Daddy says."

"So Granny's house was where Momma grew up?"

"That's right."

"What was the house like?"

"Um...It was old and big and made out of wood. It was cold, except downstairs in the big family room where the fireplace was. I slept in the attic room where Momma slept as a girl. It was cold and damp and kind of lonely. Momma slept downstairs in a room closer to Granny's room."

"What else?"

"I think there was a barn behind the house where the mean chickens lived, and there was a big black cow with white spots that Momma wanted me to milk. The cow was so big and scary, I wouldn't do it. Momma called me a scaredy-cat and squirted me in the face with milk straight from the cow. When I started crying, she laughed at me."

"Oh, no. That's not nice."

"No. It's not."

"Why do you think she did that, Maddie?"

"I guess because she's mean."

"It seems like she wasn't able to see the situation through *your* eyes, but maybe we can see it through *hers.* Do you want to try?"

She shrugs. "I guess so."

"Let's see. Your Momma grew up with cows, right?"

"Yes. She always lived in Littletown with the chickens and cows until she met Daddy."

"Maybe that thing with the cow was something she did with her friends when she was growing up. You know, friends playing in the barn, squirting each other with milk."

"But what if the cows didn't like it? What if they got mad and stepped on your foot or butted you in the head?"

"Right. That's the way you were seeing it. I probably would have seen it that way too, at your age. Unlike us, your Momma probably saw the farm critters as friends. She was probably letting you in on the game."

"I bet you're right, Tutor. I wish I'd seen it that way. I wish she'd gone slower and helped me see the fun in it."

"Yes, that would've helped, but sometimes the things we experience as children are hard to see through another person's eyes. Okay, let's get back to that other time you were afraid with Granny. Tell me more about that."

"The main thing is that she she grabbed my hand and I couldn't get loose no matter how hard I tried, and there was no one there to help me."

"How did you come to be alone with her?"

"Momma told me to stay with Granny in the bedroom while she talked to her friends. The minute she closed the door, Granny grabbed my hand and squeezed it so hard, I thought it would break. I called for Momma, but she didn't come. After that, Granny's eyes got really big, her mouth flew open, and her head fell back. She didn't move after that, but she still had my hand."

"Oh, no, Maddie. That's scary."

"Yes. Especially when nobody came to help. I didn't know what to do, Tutor. I really didn't."

"So what *did* you do?"

"I had to stay there, trying not to look at Granny's eyes. Finally, Momma came and pried my hand loose. I told her I wanted to go home, but she said we had to stay for Granny's funeral."

Tutor looks upset. "Where was Daddy all this time?"

"It wasn't his fault. He had to stay in the city for his work, but he was there when Granny was in her box at the church."

"Her box?"

"You know. Her coffin. But it was just a long box made out of wood. Momma wanted me to kiss Granny goodbye, but I wouldn't do it. I was afraid she'd grab me again. I stayed on the church bench and watched the angels flying over Jesus's head in the stained-glass scene. The angels told me I could fly away with them, if things got too bad."

"Oh, Maddie, you were so young. How do you remember all that? Most people don't form memories so clearly at that age."

"I remember it all, but when I think about the angels, it's not so scary. Momma says she loved those angels too, and she liked to watch Jesus's face to see if he was listening when the priest gave his talks."

"Was he listening?"

"I'm not sure. He looked like he might be listening, or maybe he was thinking about the baby lamb in his arms, with its curly white hair."

"That's a nice image. What else?"

"Daddy doesn't believe in all that church stuff. He says people make up God so they'll have someone to blame when things go bad, or if they need forgiveness when they've done something wrong. Do you think that's true, Tutor? Is that why people believe in God and Jesus?"

"Could be, Maddie. Fear. Uncertainty. Wanting for-giveness. A need to know what happens when we die. A hope for immortality. A need for morality. Religion pro-vides answers to those questions that can't be answered otherwise. Questions about why we die and why we were born in the first place. Questions about a bigger plan that might give some meaning to our earthly existence?" He looks away and sighs.

"Does it make you sad, Tutor?"

"Ahhh, it's just so complicated. All the things we do with our minds to comprehend the world. The stories we make up. The things we believe and defend. The things we don't believe. The only way I can make sense of it is to consider it all part of the same dream. A dream containing all of human consciousness, and lately, I've been learning about the consciousness of animals and trees, fish and flowers. Mosquitoes and bees. Beans." He grins. "It's glorious, Maddie. There are so many ways to view reality. So many personal and conceptual lenses. But it's a lot to hold all at once. Right now, I'd like to get back to your time in Littletown and think about what lessons it holds."

"I think it was a lesson about how strong people are when they die, and even after their spirit's flown away like a bird, they're still strong and they can still hold on."

"You see spirits as a birds?"

She smiles. "Why not? I bet Granny's in the top of a tree right now talking to White Bird? They're having fun."

"That's a good story. It helps you deal with what you experienced. Traumatic, formative memories have a powerful effect on us. Those scenes of you and Granny when she was dying, and the stained-glass Jesus and angels in the church seem to be crystallized in your mind. Do they ever show up in your dreams?"

"I used to have a really bad dream where I'd wake up crying."

"Can you remember how it goes?"

"I don't know if I want to remember. It's worse than any of the scary books I've read." She covers her face and peeks through her fingers. "I'll try, if you want me to."

"It might tell us something."

She takes a deep breath and lightly touches her arms to calm herself. "Okay. I think I can do it."

"Good."

"Well...sometimes, in the dream, I'd be in bed and Granny's hand would come out of the covers and grab me. Or, I'd dream about the Prince kissing me, but when I opened my eyes, it wasn't the Prince, it was Granny with her big scary eyes. If I remembered to ask the angels to watch over me before I went to sleep, Granny would stay in her coffin, and I'd go flying with the angels and not be scared."

"Maybe that's why you like flying so much. It's a way to get away when things get too hard?"

"I do like flying."

"Did Daddy have anything to say about that time in Littletown?"

"He wasn't there, except at the funeral, so he doesn't know very much."

"You never talked to him? Never told him how frightened you were by what happened with Granny, and the cow?"

"He told me it was good that I let the angels help. He said, everybody has to die, and that it was Granny's time. I asked him why she looked so scared. He said it was because of the sickness she had. He told me not everyone dies that way. Some people go gently into the dark night. I'm not sure what that means, but do you think that's true?"

"Yes, I do. Everyone's different, so why wouldn't they experience death differently? Does Momma ever talk about that time in Littletown.?"

"No, but she used to tell me old stories about Littletown, especially when she was sad and wanted to go back there. I don't know why when it's such a scary place."

"So, you're afraid of Littletown, and Momma's afraid of the city. I wonder, can you use *your* fear to help you understand *her* fear?"

She thinks about it. "Maybe. How would I do it?"

"Well, we know why you're afraid of Littletown. It's because you had a traumatic experience there. So, what traumatic experience did Momma have that made her afraid of the city?"

"I don't know, Tutor. I just know that's how she is. Sometimes she stares at the ceiling, like she's remembering something. And sometimes, she says she's lost something, but I don't know what it is. If she gets too scared, she runs upstairs to drink whiskey. There's nothing I can do to help her."

"I guess all you can do is be kind and gentle with her."

He clasps his hands behind his neck, staring up at the ceiling like he's thinking. He looks back at her. "So, Maddie. Let's talk about mind mapping, how memory works, and how we come to be who we are by way of what we hold in our memory as we live our lives. Think of the power of that memory you have of Granny. The way you saw her when she died in front of you. Her eyes wide open. Terror on her face. That's the way you'll always see her. Except wait, how did the big bad wolf get into the story? You know, with his huffing and puffing? Did you perhaps read The Three Little Pigs before you went to Littletown?"

"Probably Daddy read it to me, or maybe Momma. I think maybe she read to me when I was little. I'm not sure."

"So, I guess we could say the story of The Three Little Pigs entered the scene with Granny to help you make sense of what was happening."

"Really?"

"Could be. We always draw on what we know to make sense of the unknown, even if it makes things more scary. And now, you've got Granny's dying in your mind and it will affect your understanding and response when other people die. It might help if you could make her death less traumatic by understanding it in a new way."

Maddie frowns. "How can I do that?"

"Let's work on an easier memory first, like those mean chickens you told me about. Have you read the story of Chicken Little?"

"Yes."

"What do you think of Chicken Little?"

"I don't think she's mean. She was just trying to warn the others about the sky falling. That's not mean. It's nice. Foxy Loxy was the mean one for eating Chicken Little's friends. He shouldn't have done that. He's as bad as the bad wolf."

"So, you've got mean chickens in your mind and a nice chicken in your mind. That's a good start. What if the mean chickens only pecked your legs because they were trying to protect their eggs so they could hatch into baby chicks. What if the they were just doing what any good mother would do?"

"Really, you think that's why they pecked me?"

"Could be. How does that make you feel about the mean chickens?"

"I guess, I was the mean one. But it wasn't my fault. Momma told me to get the eggs for breakfast." She closes her eyes and whispers, "I'm sorry, chickens. I didn't know."

Tutor touches her shoulder and smiles when she opens her eyes. "It's true. You didn't know. But now you do, so you can think about the chickens in a different way. They're not mean. They're just good mothers. Can you do the same thing with Granny? Can you create a story for her that lets you see her death and your role in it in a new way?"

"I'm not sure. It might be hard."

"Right. But what if you go with the same approach? What if, instead of using the story of The Three Little Pigs, we make Granny the Granny in Little Red Riding Hood?

What if that wolf is out to hurt her and you want to help? Or, what if she's already hurting, and you want to make her feel better? What would you do?"

She thinks about it. "I guess I could touch her arms real soft, like I do to calm myself. Would that help?"

"Sure, it would. It helps to use something we know works for ourselves to help someone else. That's a start. Then, if we can put ourselves inside that other person's heart and mind and try to understand how and why they think and feel as they do, not only will it help us help them, but it will open up new ways of seeing. Empathy is powerful. Think of all the people on earth through time, each born into a unique situation. There's such a variety of ways to perceive reality. Just think what it would be like, if you could see the world through all those eyes. Think how free flying your mind would be.

Seeing and hearing another person with our senses is one thing, but empathy goes deeper. It takes into account the other person's beliefs, emotions, and experience, and if you've learned how all that works in yourself, by mapping your own mind, you'll be able to see how it works in others. Think of all you could learn from that."

He smiles. "Course, you already have a lot of that kind of empathy from trying to understand the lives of the characters in your books. You're well practiced at feeling what they feel, and thus, you understand why they do what they do. Books are good for that, and so was your experience with Granny."

"Tutor, do you think I could have helped Granny more?"

"I think you did help her. You were by her side and you held her hand when she was afraid and needed someone to hold on to. You did exactly the right thing."

"But it was so hard, Tutor. I wish you'd been there."

"Me too, Maddie. Me too. We can build that into the scene, if you like. You and me by the bed, holding hands with Granny, creating a circle of safety around her. Maybe a candle burning. Stained-glass angels hovering by."

"I like that, Tutor. I like the angels being there."

His eyes shine with a smile. "Another important thing to remember is that every time you revisit a memory, you change it. If you want to change a memory into a happier version, tell yourself a happier story. But, remember, Maddie, you don't want to get *rid* of your memories, just expand them. Without memories, life is meaningless. Your memories, and all that goes with them, are who you are."

Chapter 13

The next day, Maddie sits in her leather chair waiting for Tutor to begin his lesson. He takes a quick breath, leans forward with one elbow on his knee, his chin in his hand. "So, Maddie. How about a lesson on something a little less abstract than our previous lessons?"

"Okay."

"Let's take a geometric view of things, you know, where space is defined by the hard edges of shapes such as triangles, rectangles, and squares. Or circles, which are soft and round and infinite. No sharp edges on a circle. You can hold it in your arms. You can bounce it. But that would be a sphere, wouldn't it?"

Maddie shrugs. "Umm…I guess so."

"I mean, a sphere is just a circle blown out in all directions around a central point, like a balloon, or a basketball. But that would take us into three dimensions where triangles become pyramids and squares become cubes. Things get more geometrically and psychologically complex in the three dimensional world." He waggles his head, telling her he knows he's talking over her head. "So, what do you know about geometry, Maddie?"

She frowns. "Not a whole lot. Daddy stopped teaching me when Momma got sick."

"She got sick?"

"Yes. She kept throwing up, and she was really sad. That's when she got mad at Daddy and made him sleep in a different room. It was like…I don't know." She slaps her hand over her mouth, whimpering, "I can't think about that, Tutor. It's too sad. I want to be happy."

"I know, Maddie. I know. That's why I suggested geometry. I thought it was safe, but I guess even geometry can hurt when it reminds us of something else." He looks at the floor, then back at her with sad eyes. "Okay. Let's start over. What *did* you learn about geometry before Daddy stopped teaching you?"

"I just learned about the shapes. You know, the triangles and squares, like you said. And he told me about numbers and how wide things are, like where the triangle comes to a point, or that special number that says the distance around a circle."

"You mean, Pi?"

"Yes. That's it. Pi, like a cherry pie or a pizza pie." She smirks. "I don't know how it all works with the balls and balloons and things, and I didn't know about the cubes and pyramids. Wait. Are you talking about the pyramids in Egypt?"

"You know about those, huh?"

"Of course, I do. I want to go to Egypt and see them."

"I'd like to see them too."

She claps. "Okay then, let's do it."

"Righto! I'll put it on my calendar." He pulls an imaginary calendar from his pocket and writes it down.

Maddie does the same thing. "Good. Now teach me about the shapes?"

"Sure. Geometry is all about dimensions, right?"

She doesn't know if that's true, but she nods.

"A line only has length, which makes it one-dimensional. Shapes such as squares, triangles, and circles have width and length, but no depth, which means they're flat.

Shapes like spheres, pyramids, cylinders, and cones have three dimensions: height, width, and depth. Those shapes have a more complex psychological effect on us. They give us a sense of strength and endurance. You might feel like you can push over a three line triangle or a four line square, but it's not as easy with a pyramid or a cube. Depth carries weight, it gives objects a sense of presence and permanence. Our environment is full of three-dimensional objects to which we attach meaning and value."

Maddie frowns. "I'm sorry, Tutor. I didn't hear everything you said. I was still trying to push over the triangles."

He laughs and rolls his eyes. "Right. Okay. Let's simplify things. What comes to mind when you see a line?"

She shrugs. "I don't know. It's just a line. You know. A straight mark on the paper or the wall."

"Yes. A basic shape from which other shapes are constructed."

She smiles. "Right. But you know, there's something else it could be."

"What's that?"

"It could be the line between the opposites. You know, up and down. Or left and right. It could even be a line between you and me, that's sometimes too long."

Tutor slaps his leg and whoops. "Oh great. You've spoiled my lesson."

"I'm sorry! I'm sorry!" She slaps her own leg to play along.

"No. Don't be sorry. You raised the issue of the psychological qualities of the spaces we find ourselves in with others, and how we perceive that space in personal terms, such as, side-by-side. Too close. Too far away, and sometimes, perfect. What you said was brilliant." He smiles, then goes silent.

"Thank you, Tutor, I'm glad you think I'm brilliant, but what else can you teach me about the shapes?"

"Well, I was saying how solid shapes carry more psychological weight than simple lines, but once again, you've shown me how a single line can have deep psychological meaning as well, like that line between you and me, or the line between you *up* in the condo and the playground *down* below. The line that made you feel left out. That made you want to fly like a bird so you could join the kids on the swings. But you never could. You experienced an up and down line that brought sadness and frustration." His eyes fill with tears. "Dear Maddie, I've missed your lessons."

She gasps. "Really, I give you lessons?"

"Of course. As I've said before, you developed a wide and varied perspective from living out the lives of the characters in your books. Seeing how things look and feel from all sides. You know what it's like to be Jack as well as Jill. David as well as Goliath. That's why you were quick to understand the concept of looking through different lenses. You already had a myriad of lenses in your mind that you were adept at seeing through. It's made you empathetic and wise."

"Really, Tutor?"

"Yes. Really. Most people have interactions with many people as they go through life: parents and teachers, siblings and friends. Babysitters. People they meet on the street or at the store. All those encounters shape them, and to a large degree, determine who they are and how they perceive and behave in the world.

You haven't had those kinds of influence. You mostly brought yourself up, like I did. We both filled in the meaning of our experiences in life and gained understanding of the world and other people from the books we read. No one told us what to focus on, or what the right answers were. We got our answers by playing out the lives of the different characters, learning how each perceived the world. As a result, we've gathered a lot of ideas and concepts over the years. That's why we're eclectic."

"I don't know what that means."

"An eclectic person has a mind composed of many concepts. And remember how I said we can fly higher and faster when we think conceptually? We can try one concept after the next, letting our heads spin without getting bogged down in all the details. We've both got minds like that. We don't lose our balance when our heads are spinning." He wobbles his head. "We like entering those worlds of the unknown."

"That's right. We do. So, you're saying we're the same?"

He smiles. "Yes, Maddie, we are."

"I like that, Tutor."

"I believe Big Daddy brought us together because he saw right away that we were made of the same cloth." He smirks. "You know, paisley or plaid."

Maddie sniggers. "Or maybe pink polka dots on black taffeta." She points to a dot on her skirt.

"Exactly. We both know what we see in a given moment is just one way of seeing it. Our eclecticism gives us a head start when it comes to quickly switching conceptual lenses. Many people wouldn't know how to do it, or even what I'm talking about, but you do."

"That's right. I do." She sparkles her eyes and smiles.

Tutor sparkles his eyes and smiles back, then gets serious. "Maddie. A person can get trapped in a narrow view of reality by way of the lessons they learn through life, the things they were reinforced to believe in their early years, and continue to believe over time. They reach a point where they believe that what they believe *is* absolutely true, without question. If you want to free yourself from that kind of narrow view, you'll need to learn how your mind is constructed and how it works. Then fill it with all kinds of new knowledge and watch what happens."

She thinks about it. "How do I find out how my mind works?"

"The best way to understand your mind is to map it."

"You talked about that before, but what does it mean, exactly, and how do I do it?"

"You map your mind by tracing back through your memories to see where your emotions and beliefs were born. When you think something you think is true, without question, track it back to where you first established that truth. Then, follow the rippling effects of the belief up through time, focusing on how it has influenced your perception and behavior over time. Look deeply into how your all your beliefs operate in your life, for good or bad, and if there's no benefit, leave them behind."

Maddie shakes her head in amazement. "How did you learn all these things, Tutor?"

He laughs. "That's a good question. I guess it started when I realized I was blaming my father and Mum for everything bad in my life. I believed it was their fault that I was living in a basement room in the library without company of any kind. It was true. If they hadn't done what *they* did, I wouldn't have been in that situation, and I wouldn't be who I was.

I felt justified in my blame, but then I realized I could go my whole life blaming them, or I could accept responsibility for myself and gain some freedom. What I had in my head, the things I believed, the things I wanted to be true, even that blame I had for my parents, created the world I lived in. If I wanted to change my world, I needed to understand things in a new way. I had to stop handing the power off to someone else who wasn't even there anymore.

I wanted to be in charge, Maddie. I wanted to know that whoever I was it was of my own making. Nobody else was to blame, nor could they take credit."

He frowns. "No. That's not true. They can take some credit and blame, but I don't hold that as the only truth. It puts me in a narrow place where I don't want to live. So, Maddie, what do you say, should we get started mapping *your* mind?"

She punches the air with both hands. "Yes!"

"Okay. Let's see." He moves his head back and forth in a bouncy way like he's listening to music, then he stops and looks her in the eye. "Okay, try this. What is your first memory of fear?"

"Fear?"

"Yes. Fear is a powerful emotion that affects perception and behavior at a very deep level. So, when were you first *really* afraid?"

The answer comes quick. "It was when Granny died. When she held my hand real tight and wouldn't let go."

"Yes, that's a scary one. Can you remember what thoughts came along with that fear?"

She shakes her hair over her face to think. When the answer comes, she flips it back. "The scariest thing was being alone and not knowing what to do. Daddy wasn't there and Momma was with her friends on the porch. There was no one to help me and it seems like it happened before."

"When was that?"

"Um…I'm not sure."

"At the condo?"

"Yes. That's it. It was when Momma was really sick and scared and Daddy was on one of his long business trips so he couldn't help. Momma stayed in bed the whole time, so I was completely alone. That was before Mim and White Bird came, so I didn't have anyone to talk to. The silence got so big, I had to cover my ears but I could still hear it screaming. I didn't know what to do."

"What *did* you do?"

"I don't know. I might have read my books, or maybe I was too young. I can't remember. Maybe I had some picture books, or some easier ones." She doesn't want to think about it. "What's your first memory of fear, Tutor."

"Hmmm. I guess it's the same with me as for you. I know that kind of loneliness you describe, and I've heard that screaming silence. When my father went off to war, it brought an unbearable emptiness to the house. Then my mother left and the silence started screaming. That felt like fear."

"That kind of silence really scares me, Tutor. But after you came, I didn't hear it as much. I knew you'd be back the next day. I'd think of things I wanted to tell you, so it was like we were talking the whole time. Then Momma made you go away, and I thought I'd never see you again, and–."

She stops to catch her breath. "I'm sorry, Tutor, what were you saying?"

"Interesting how emotions bring back memories, and memories bring back emotions. One following the next, rippling through time. The more you map those ripples back and forth through time, the more you'll know who you are and how you came to be who you are."

"I'd like to know who I am, Tutor. I really would."

Chapter 14

Maddie stands next to Tutor at the window in Daddy's study watching the cotton candy clouds sail across the sky. He nudges her arm. "What do you see out there?"

"Clouds."

"What else?"

"Birds that aren't there."

"Yes. An absence. They're interesting, aren't they? What else?"

"Skyscrapers. But they're always the same. Except in the evening when the sunset reflects in the high windows making them blaze red and gold, or in the morning, when the bright white light glitters like diamonds around the hanging window washers."

"Oh, yes, sunsets and window washers. Two more things that aren't there."

She thinks of something else he might like. "I see bears too."

"Really?"

"Yes. They gallop down the side of the mountain like wild horses." She grabs his hand with a pretend scared look in her eyes. "I can't stop them, Tutor. They're going to gallop off the cliff into the ocean. They'll drown."

His eyes widen. "Quick. Jump on their backs. Rein those babies in."

She giggles and slaps his hand. "You, silly. I just made that up. Anyways, it's from a dream I have sometimes... about bears...and other things."

He thumps himself in the forehead, like he's embarrassed he believed her about the bears for even a second, then he rocks his head from side to side and smiles. "You realize you've done that thing again, don't you?"

"What thing?"

"You replaced what's happening now with a figment of your imagination. You whisked us right out of the present moment."

Maddie gasps. "Oh, no. I'm sorry, Tutor. I didn't mean to. Sometimes, it just happens."

"Don't be sorry, Maddie. It's normal. We all do it. It's what being human is all about. We take the present moment and overlay it with meaning from the past, each in our own way."

"Even you, Tutor?"

"Sure, but the absences aren't birds and wild bears for me. My father and my Mum are the absences in my life."

"That's right. They died like Granny?"

"Yes. They did." He sighs, turns from the window, and looks around the study. "Maddie, do you think we can experience this room as it is right now, in this moment, without overlaying meaning from the past or future."

She looks around. "It seems like we could."

"Okay. Let's try." He moves his hand over her head and whispers in a low voice, "Let your thoughts fly away like a feather on a breeze. Breathe in. Breathe out. Listen to the silence. Focus only on what's here."

She realizes how dark and gloomy the study is. They should turn on the lamp. The stained-glass fruit would glow and make things cheerful.

Oh no. She did it again. She was thinking about the glow that's missing.

Tutor holds up a finger. "It's okay. Close your eyes and listen. Just listen."

She closes her eyes and pretty soon she hears the soft whisper of Tutor's breath, then the low murmur of her own breath. Listening helps the thoughts stay away, but then the silence gets loud, like it does when it's late at night and she's worried Daddy won't come home. Which means she'll be trapped inside the condo forever, alone, with Momma.

She shakes her head, trying to escape that thought. "It's really hard, Tutor. My mind keeps thinking of those things that aren't here. I can't make it stop."

"Like I said, Maddie. It's perfectly normal."

"If it's so normal, why do we have to stop doing it? I mean, why do you want me to stop having thoughts and just see and hear the room?"

"Good question, Maddie. Thing is, I'm trying to help you see how thoughts complicate what you see with your senses. The absences you see in your mind, the birds, the bears, the sunsets of yesterday, they're all elements drawn from experiences you've had in your life. Each absence is a ghost from your past. These ghosts are involved in creating your perception. They make meaning out of the stream of things that happen in your life, but they also pull you out of the moment you're in, so you can't experience it fully. The past creates the future, often side-stepping the now. It's not good or bad, Maddie. It's just how it is. It's good to understand how it works."

She frowns. She's heard every word he said, but she still doesn't know how the absences work, and whether it's a good thing or a bad thing to see them.

"Think about it this way, Maddie. You might think that when two people look at the same pine tree they see the same tree. But that's generally not true. If one of them had the experience of wandering in the dappled shade of the giant Sequoias of California, that pine tree might look quite small and insignificant. On the other hand, if a person had a pine tree smash through their roof on a windy night in the rain, that pine tree might look big and foreboding. Can you see how experience effects what each one perceives?"

She nods. "Yes, I can see how that works. I wonder how experience makes me see you."

"I don't know. How *do* you see me?"

She would say the Mad Hatter, but he's not like that anymore. He's more serious now, more like she imagines a teacher from the real world would be.

He catches her eye. "The thing to remember is that we perceive the world through the lens of the experiences of our life. Some experiences are low key, but gain power through repetition. Other experiences are so powerful they cause an instant change in our beliefs and perception when they happen. In the end, we're like the characters in your books. We each have a series of personal stories that determine how we perceive and respond to the moments of our lives. You could say we exist within the stream of our constant whispering stories."

His words take her back to when she realized she wasn't living in her book stories anymore. Is that what he means? Is he saying that when he came to teach her it was so powerful she entered the real world and left the book characters behind? She claps her hands. "I think I know what you mean, Tutor."

"That's great. What do I mean?"

"You mean, when something big happens you don't have to live inside the old stories anymore. Like what happened to me, when you came."

"Yes. That's it. Exactly. Come, let's sit. I'll tell you a story about one of those big formative events in my life."

They go back to their leather chairs.

Tutor runs his fingers through his dark hair, he takes a deep breath, and lets it out with his first word. "Okay. I guess the best place to start is where it started. When my father was about the same age as I am now, married to his sweetheart, Mum, with a young son, me. He got caught up in the current war, enlisted, and never came home. Or, more precisely, he came home in a black plastic bag."

"Why would he do that?"

"Because he died in that war."

"That's right. You told me that. I'm so sorry, Tutor."

"That's war, Maddie. Not everyone dies, but even if they don't, they're not the same afterwards. Some are destroyed by physical wounds, others by wounds of the heart or mind. Some just go numb. And then, there's the collateral damage."

She doesn't know what *co-la-teral* means, but she's too sad to ask.

He touches her shoulder. "I'm not trying to make you sad, Maddie. I'm just trying to tell you about my life. How it set me in a direction, taught me what I know about the world, and made me who I am to a large degree. It's a lesson."

"Okay. I'll try not to be sad."

Tutor sighs. "After my father died, Mum turned to drink and magic. She'd change from the Queen of Hearts to the Ace of Spades in an instant, then she'd vanish into thin air and reappear days later, as if she was never gone. She'd stock the house up with food, then disappear again. She came and went so many times, I never knew if she'd be there or not when I got home from school.

Then one night, she turned into a thin sliver of silver light, slipped through a crack in the night, and I never saw her again."

"Oh no, Tutor. That must have been so hard. Where did she go?"

He shrugs. "I don't know. I waited for her to come home, but she never did. I hid from the school people when they came looking for me. Hid from the police. Then I heard some men talking about clearing out the house so it could be sold. I grabbed what I could and left without being seen.

I found a secret room under the city library that nobody used. It had a cement floor, with an old Chinese rug and a narrow cot. That's where I stayed, for a long time. At night, I'd sneak up into the library to read, working my way from one bookshelf to the next, learning as much as I could. I wanted to know everything, hoping it would help me understand what happened with my father and my Mum. I wanted to know why they did what they did and how they came to be who they were. Those are the lessons I'm trying to teach you now."

His eyes flit back and forth, sparking blue, then turning black, just before they disappear behind his closed lids.

She wonders if he's gone to sleep, but then his eyes pop open and he continues. "Being alone like that, I cried. I felt sad for myself. I was hungry. I was angry. Confused. Lonely. Depressed. Proud that I could survive on my own. The books were my friends, my teachers. Every one I read gave me another perspective of the world. They helped me understand my situation. My father. My Mum. Myself. I experienced every human emotion there is, watching myself the whole time, talking to myself, learning from myself. When I'd learned everything I could from being alone with the books, I went up to live on the streets to see what I could learn there."

She grabs his hand. "How could you do that, Tutor? How could you be all alone for so long?"

He shakes his head in a way that makes her think he wonders the same thing. "I'm like you, I guess. A survivor. You don't have enough freedom, and I had too much freedom."

He gazes at her with sad eyes. "Having magic helped. I got that from Mum. Watching her change from the kindest person in all the world, to a wild thing flying around the house. She frightened me and amazed me. I loved her, and I'm sure she loved me in her own sad way, but she didn't know how to be with me after my father died. I reminded her too much of him and what she'd lost. I don't know where she ended up, or even if she's still alive. Thing is, Maddie, she was my Mum, but she had her own story to live, like everyone. A sad story in her case."

"It's the saddest story I've ever heard. I feel so bad for you, Tutor. And her, and your father."

"But, Maddie. I've learned so much from my life. I wouldn't trade it for all the world."

"Well, I wish I could've been there to be your friend like you are for me."

His eyes glisten. "That would've been really nice. Turns out, I did find a friend."

"You did?"

"Yes. When I went up to live on the streets, I learned to juggle and do card tricks to survive. I pulled coins out of people's ears. When I didn't have coins, I pulled out rocks."

He pulls a little round rock from her ear and hands it to her. "I got so good at slight of hand, I took to stealing people's watches and wallets. I'm not proud of that. But that was how I met my…guardian angel, I guess you'd call him. I stole his wallet, but he was sneakier than me. He stole it right back while we were walking to a restaurant where he was going to buy me lunch. We talked and laughed about his wallet. Then he took me home to meet his wife. She was just as nice as he was. At fourteen, I suddenly had a room of my own in a beautiful house, breakfast in the morning, dinner at night. It's unbelievable what the world can deliver to you, Maddie. Remember that. Anything is possible."

"I believe it, Tutor. An impossible thing happened when you came to teach me and now, even though Momma tried to stop it, you're back."

"Exactly. Events happen in our lives, some good, some bad. You need to understand how it all comes together to make you who you are. Listen to your thoughts. See how they affect the way you perceive things. When you have a strong emotion, track it back to it's source in your life story. If you want to change something, create a different version of the story, like we did with Granny and the mean chickens, that weren't mean. Once you've mapped your mind, in this way, you'll not only understand yourself better, you'll understand others too. You'll know how the human mind is put together and what it means to be human. Mind is everything, Maddie. Learn how to see what it's doing, then, let it fly."

"I'll try, Tutor. I like flying."

"That's one thing I know for sure about you." He stands. "Now, Maddie, I'm sorry to say, I have to go."

She's about to protest, but she knows it won't do any good. When it's time to go, he goes.

Chapter 15

The next morning, Tutor paces while Maddie picks at the pleats on her yellow-and-white daisy dress.

He stops in front of her. "So, Maddie. I told you my story about war. What else do you know about war?"

She shrugs. "A few things, I guess...from Daddy's book."

"What book are we talking about?"

"It's called *The History of the Whole World*. It has lots of stories about everything, including wars."

"Really? You read *that*?"

She fluffs her hair. "Some of it...or maybe Daddy was the one reading. Maybe that's why I can't remember everything...about war."

"That's okay. What *do* you remember?"

"You know, things about the American wars. The civil one, and the one for our independence. George Washington and Paul Revere were in that one. I also know about the World Wars and the fall of the Roman's Empire, and Cleopatra, but that was from the movie I saw on Momma's TV, and it's not really about war. Is it?"

Tutor strikes a glamorous pose. "Oh, yes, Cleopatra. She was something, wasn't she? Queen of the Nile. A real charmer. Spoke a dozen languages. Educated in mathematics, philosophy, and public speaking. But she wasn't the beauty Elizabeth Taylor would have you believe. No. It wasn't her *physical* qualities that made her so...popular. It was her *mellifluous* voice and *irresistible* charm." He smiles and ends his pose.

Maddie stares into the blue amethyst shine of his eyes, trying to remember what he just said.

He blinks and his eyes go dark. "But let's not get side-tracked on Cleopatra. I was about to tell you about Genghis Khan." He pulls a piece of folded paper from his coat pocket and flourishes it in the air like a fan.

Maddie expects a white dove to fly out, but it doesn't.

"Come," he says, "let's take a look at this old map." He goes to Daddy's desk and spreads it out.

She stands by his side and watches him wag his finger over the map.

"What is it, Tutor?"

"All of the red is Genghis Khan's empire at its height. He conquered a good half of the known world of his time. Destroyed property and culture, killed something like forty million people. All that turmoil and violence, all that riding around on horses, setting fires, killing folks. In the end, his kingdom only lasted a hundred years. What does that tell you about war, Maddie?"

"It tells me a lot of people have to die, but it doesn't do any good."

"Yes. You could say that. So why do people *do* it?"

She's about to answer, but he holds up a finger. "Genghis Khan was a murderously mean man in battle. He and his soldiers didn't give a hoot about who they killed, men, women, children…old grannies. Then, after the battle was over, he was nice as pie to the people who survived. He said if they were loyal to him they wouldn't have to die. He wouldn't have their heads chopped off or drag them behind a wild horse until they were torn up and bleeding."

"Ugh. That's awful. Why was he so mean?"

"Why, indeed? Let's think about it."

They go back to their chairs. "Listen, Maddie. Here's something most people don't know about Genghis Khan. It's strange, but he liked to collect one smooth stone and the right middle finger of every person he personally killed at each battle. He let ants and bugs clean the finger bones, then he put the stones and bones into beautiful carved wooden boxes with insets of the gold, silver, and turquoise his army had stolen along the way. When each box was full, he'd have it sent off by pony express to be stored in an old outbuilding at his mother's house.

When the warring ended, he went home and had his mason build a long wall out of the smooth stones. The first full moon, Genghis went out and scattered the finger bones along the length of the wall. Think about it, Maddie. It wasn't a wall that held anything in, or anything out, just a long smooth stone wall frosted with a glistening layer of middle finger bones from his hundred-year war."

"That's horrible! It's as bad as that witch who kept checking Hansel's finger to see if he was fat enough to eat."

"Right, but Hansel was one smart cookie. He found a skinny finger bone from another boy she'd already eaten —"

Maddie shouts, "That's right. He stuck that finger bone out instead of his own finger, and it tricked the witch into feeding him more cookies and letting him live longer."

"Yes, but eventually, she would have eaten him and Gretel too, if Gretel hadn't pushed her into the oven. In this story, the girl's the real hero."

"That's right. And in the end, Hansel and Gretel took the witch's pearls and precious stones and went home. By then, the mean step-mother, who took them to the forest in the first place, was dead, and the father was really happy to see them."

Tutor sits back and runs his finger over his lips. "It's interesting you brought up that old fairy tale. It reminded me of the finger bones in my story about Genghis Khan. By the way, did you think that Genghis story was true?"

"Of course, I did. Shouldn't I?"

He shakes his head. "No, Maddie. You shouldn't. It's a *good* story, but truth is, I made the whole thing up just now."

She stares at him in disbelief. "Why, Tutor? Why would you try to make me believe something that's not true?"

"So you'll think about everything you hear, Maddie. Decide for yourself if it's true. That way, you can't be hood-winked by the likes of me or anyone else."

"I don't even know what hoodwinked means."

"It means any number of things, deceived, tricked, duped, cheated, defrauded, deluded. Take your pick."

"So, it's not a *good* thing?"

"No, Maddie. It's not."

"Then why do people do it?"

He tugs his little beard. "For several reasons. One, to make you believe things so you'll think and behave in a certain way. And two, so they can get something from you, money, power, a sense of being smarter, stronger, better, or funnier, than you. Actually, there are all kinds of reasons why people might try to hoodwink you with a good story. Fact is, we're fed stories from the day we're born. Stories about God and country. Stories about Grandma, *Alice in Wonderland*. Peter Pan. The Man in the Moon…Where'd *he* come from?"

He smirks. "Listen, Maddie, as I've said before, the world we know and understand is constructed from the stories we've been told all our lives. That, and stories we tell ourselves and believe. Some stories, we all believe. Stories about the basic laws of nature or the fact that we're all human, and what that means at the most basic level. Other stories are bound to a particular culture, religion, or period of time. For example, how do you think people view Genghis Khan these days?"

She shrugs. "I'm not sure. It seems like they'd still think he's mean for killing all those people."

"It depends on where you live and what stories you've been told. In Mongolia, Genghis Khan is a national hero, whereas in Russia, school children are taught that Khan and his Mongols were occupiers that brought only pain and suffering. Some historians say Khan and his Mongols committed every military atrocity ever perpetrated by man. Others say his campaign of terror was a good thing because it brought peace among the various tribes that had been killing each other for hundreds of years. Once the fighting was over, Genghis treated all people equally. He adopted enemy orphans and prisoners and gave them all work. He opened up the Silk Road from China, which brought exotic products to the people for the first time. Spices, silk, the printing press."

"So, you're saying, in some ways, he's good. But what about all the people that died?"

"Yes, what about them?" He lifts a shoulder and lets it fall with a sigh. "Maddie, you and I don't have an investment in what to believe about Genghis Khan. He didn't kill our loved ones. Nor did he bring us peace and prosperity after a long terrible period of war. We've just got distant, contradicting stories to sort through. Stories that have changed over time. How can we know the truth?"

"It seems like we should be able to know the truth. Otherwise, how can we know what to believe."

"Yes, we do have to *believe* we know the truth sometimes. For example, when we're trying to make a decision in the moment in order to act. Otherwise, we *can't* act. Turn left? Turn right? We have to make that decision, or we're not going to get anywhere. But in many cases, like with Genghis Khan, truth is in the eye of the beholder. Or as Einstein would say, it's all relative. Whether you accept the slipperiness of truth or you hang tight to a particular version of it, there will still be times when you have to deal with not knowing what's true. It's a fact of life. So, you might as well learn how to ride that wild horse of not knowing with open eyes and a free mind."

"I'm not sure what horse you're talking about. Can it fly?"

"Certainly it can. I'm talking about the wild flying horse of the unknown. Admitting you don't know is a good place to start. Learn to let truth slide while you consider all the angles and look for truth at the deepest levels."

He looks at her with dark eyes. "By the way, what's the deeper truth in Hansel and Gretel. I mean, what does that story say about real people and real life?"

Maddie picks at the pleats on her dress while she thinks. "Well, it seems like it's saying mothers want everything for themselves. They're mean, and don't care if the children get lost in the forest and die, but fathers are nice. He loves his children and he wants them to be happy."

"That sounds like a familiar story, but there's more to it than that. Right?"

"Um...sometimes it's probably true that mothers *don't* want their children around because they're too noisy or they keep asking to do things she doesn't want them do. She might want to send them to the forest for some peace and quiet. But I think if the children could go out and play sometimes, they'd be happy and wouldn't cause any trouble. They could learn to do things for themselves, so the mother wouldn't have to tell them they're wrong all the time. Is that the kind of deeper truth you're asking about?"

"Yes. You could say Hansel and Gretel is a fairy tale about the selfishness of adults, the cleverness of children, and the kind of evil that arises in difficult times, such as famine."

Maddie gasps. "That's right! The wicked mother sent the children away because she was hungry, and the old witch wanted to eat the children so she must have been hungry too. It's all about being hungry, isn't it? I never thought of it like that."

Tutor smiles. "Oh. That's good, Maddie. At first, you personalized the story, and now you see it in a different way. That's how it works. Like I said before, we encounter stories and experiences in the world, and we add them to what we already hold in our minds. Each new experience affects the earlier ones, but some powerful experiences have a really strong hold on us, and they don't change much, despite what new experience tells us. Those deeply ingrained experiences have the strongest influence over our beliefs and perceptions. They shape the stories we rely on when making choices and navigating the world." It's especially important to analyze those stories." He stands and goes to the window.

She's about to join him when he comes back. "What I'm trying to say is that once a story gets hold of you, and you take it as truth, you lose a certain degree of freedom. You stop seeing things as an open question to explore.

Try to gather a variety of experiences and conceptual options so you can see the world through a prism lens, where different levels of truth are simultaneously at play. In other words, reach for the whole enchilada. As Albert Einstein once said, '*Any fool can know. The point is to understand.*'"

He opens the study door, then looks back with a smile. "Today, I told you a formative story of my life. Tomorrow, you can tell me one from yours."

She frowns. "But I don't have any stories, except the ones you've already heard. Remember, I've been stuck here in this condo my whole life."

"I'm sure you'll think of something, Maddie. Bye, now. Sweet dreams."

With a wave of his hand, he's gone.

Chapter 16

Maddie can't sleep. Her mind's too busy trying to think of a good story to tell Tutor. She needs something with magic, like the one about his Mum disappearing into the sliver of light.

She could tell him about Mim and how she first appeared as a flicker of light in the steamy bathroom mirror, then showed up again in the black lacquer mirror. That was the proof that the mirror really was magic, like Daddy said. Mim came all the time after that. She grew so bright, they could touch noses through the glass. She used to wish she could enter Mim's world, but now she doesn't want that. She's got Tutor in the real world.

She tries to think of something besides Mim, but her stories are all boring. The only fun she had before Tutor came was living out the stories of the fairy tale people, or pretending she was one of the birds in Daddy's Audubon book, or maybe an elephant. She likes elephants, and she really likes zebras, but she doesn't have any stories about them. By morning, she still doesn't have a good story to tell.

When Tutor arrives, they go to the study. He closes and locks the door, then they settle into their big leather chairs, smiling at each other.

Tutor sparkles his eyes and says, "So?"

She scowls. "So, *what*?"

"Are you ready to tell me a formative story from your life?"

"No," she shouts. "I don't have a life, so how could I have a story?" She clamps a hand over her mouth, wondering why she feels so mad.

"It's okay, Maddie. There's no special requirement for your story. We're just talking about stories you've got in your mind. It doesn't matter if they come from the outside world or this inside world where you live."

"Okay." She tries to think of something, anything. "The only thing I have that's any good is that dream I keep having. But dreams aren't real, so they don't count. *Do they?*"

"Sure, they do. Especially recurring dreams. Dreams have a powerful effect on the way we see the world. If you're confused about something, dreams can help you make sense of it. In that way, dreams affect perception. That's what we're talking about here, right? The power of experience, even in dreams, to affect the way we perceive the world?"

She nods. "Okay."

Tutor smiles and sends a sprinkling of white light from his ears.

She giggles. "What was that?"

He acts like he doesn't know what she's talking about. "So, Maddie, tell me about that dream of yours. What's it about?"

"A house."

"Oh, that's good. What kind of house?"

"A strange house. On the side of a mountain."

"What mountain is that?"

"I don't know. Just a mountain."

"What else can you tell me about this dream house of yours?"

"The house doesn't have a door so you can only enter from above. You fly above it, point your toes straight down, and zoom in through the roof."

"Interesting. No door. I wonder why that is."

She smirks. "I guess it's to keep people out that can't fly. Or maybe it's where the secrets are kept, so it has to be safe." She tries to think of something else in the dream he'd like. "The main room is dark and empty, but there's a tall glass of orange juice on the table. It's brighter than any orange juice I've ever seen. Like there's a light inside it. Like the glowing light inside the oranges and grapes in Daddy's stained-glass lamp. I don't drink the juice, because I like how it shines, and it's the only color in the mostly gray dream." She thinks. "Well, except the bears, they have color, but they're outside."

"That's right. You mentioned those galloping bears before. What are they like?"

"They're big, brown Grizzly bears with humps on their backs and bright yellow eyes. The mountainside is green, with white and pink flowers, and bees flying every which way, gathering pollen. There's that ocean too, at the bottom of the cliffs. I've only seen it once, but it has raging white waves that crash on the black rocks in a scary way. Everything outside the house has color, but inside, there's only the orange juice surrounded by those shadowy grays between black and white like you talked about before. You know, the grays between the black and white opposites."

He smiles and nods. "Yes. The grays. The inbetween zone of the opposites. You say there's an ocean in this dream?"

"Yes. It's scary. The Grizzly bears are galloping toward the cliff above the ocean. I don't want them to die, but there's no door, so I can't get outside to warn them."

Tutor whispers, "Kind of like you not having a door here."

"Yes." Tears come to her eyes when she realizes Tutor understands.

"Do you know why you want to save those bears, Maddie? Some people might be afraid of them."

"They shouldn't have to die just because they don't know there's a cliff. And besides, sometimes, bears are nice."

He catches her eye. "Who are these bears?"

She shrugs. "They're just bears."

"I mean, who is it you think you have to save?"

At first, she's not sure, but then she knows who it is. "It's me. I have to save myself. If I ever get to go out into the world, I won't know where the cliffs are. I won't know anything about the world. It might be dangerous. But that makes me sound like Momma, and I don't want to be a scaredy cat like she is. I'd rather go off the cliff with the bears and find out what happens. I'm sure White Bird would come to save me. He'd help me fly, and we'd go someplace fun."

"Maybe you and White Bird could teach those Grizzlies how to fly. That way, you wouldn't have to worry about them crashing on the rocks."

"Really? Do you think we could?"

"Sure. Why not? Anything can happen in a dream."

She smiles and pats his knee. "Okay, I'm going to ask White Bird to help."

"Good. Now let's see. You said there's a window in this house, but no door."

"No outside door, but there's one inside the main room. Sometimes it's there, and sometimes it's not. When it's there, I can go through to a long hall with more doors on each side. If I try to open any of those doors, I end up back in the main room with the orange juice."

"Does it frighten you when that happens?"

Maddie nods. "It gets too quiet, like there's nobody left in the whole world. Then I hear something, but I'm not sure what it is."

"What kind of something?"

"Maybe a growl, or the howl of a mad tiger, or a lonely wolf. Maybe it's just silence screaming, like it does. Sometimes I hear a baby crying. I think I've heard that cry in the real world...but that can't be true, can it?"

"I don't know, was there ever a baby in the real world?"

"I don't think so. But maybe there *was* one when I was little. When I first heard it cry in the dream, I asked Momma if the baby was real. She got mad and yelled, 'No,' but sometimes she lies. I asked Daddy too, but he said, 'That's a complicated story for later.' So I'm not sure if the baby was real or just in my dream."

"Maybe both." Tutor gets up and goes to the window. He looks out for a minute and comes back with a question. "Is that dream baby a boy or a girl?"

"How could I know? It was just crying behind one of the doors."

"And you never thought about whether it was a boy or a girl?"

"Well, it might have been a boy."

"And do you think the real baby, if there was a real baby, was a boy?"

"It seems like it. But it's hard to tell when its wrapped in a blanket, isn't it?"

"You saw it wrapped in a blanket?"

"Well, if it was real, I might have. I'm not sure."

Tutor takes a quick breath and spikes his hair. "Are there any books in this dream?"

"What? No. My books are all in the real world."

"Are there any birds?"

"I don't think so. Is that important?"

"Not really. I was just thinking how much you like birds, but I guess you're the bird in this dream."

She hoots and claps her hands. "That's right. I'm the bird that flies to the house in my white princess dress. I'm the one who points my toes down and zooms in through the roof." She stands and swirls her skirt. "This is the dress I was wearing when I went flying with White Bird."

"Really?"

"Yes." She sees the brown stains and explains, "It's not dirty like this in the dream, and I don't have to use my cloth wings. I just magically fly to the house, point my toes down, and zoom inside." She gives him a little bow. "Do you like my story, Tutor. It has magic, like yours."

"Yes, Maddie. I like it a lot. It's an important story. I think you should try to find out what's inside those rooms behind the closed doors in the hall."

"Really? I'm kind of scared of those rooms, Tutor. What if I end up with the tiger or the wolf? Or what if I find the baby, and I don't know how to make him stop crying?"

"You'll know what to do when you get there. I bet those rooms hold some very interesting clues about you. If you like, I can teach you how to walk down that hall and open the doors, even if they're locked."

"Really? You can do that?"

"Yes. If you're willing."

"Okay. But why does it scare me so much?"

"Because it's the unknown. There's nothing more unknown than the self when you first start to explore it. And there's nothing grander than meeting yourself and shaking hands once you understand who you are in all your complex dimensions."

Maddie's not sure what he means, but she doesn't care. He liked her story, and he didn't seem bored at all. Maybe she *should* try to find out what's behind the doors or take a sip of the orange juice to see what happens. Maybe it would change things in a good way, like the cake in *Alice in Wonderland*. Maybe with Tutor's help, the magic orange juice will help her find out if the crying baby is real.

Chapter 17

Maddie's in bed fighting her frustration. No matter how many times she takes a deep breath and lets it out slow, she can't calm herself. Even touching her arms real soft doesn't work. She needs Tutor so bad. She's been trying to get through the locked doors in her dream house to find out if the baby is real, but she can't do it. She needs Tutor's help, but he won't be back until Monday.

Daddy's on one of his long trips to Japan. That means it's just her and Momma, and Momma's probably waiting for her to come down for breakfast. She better go.

She slips on a pretty blue dress and runs downstairs, where she finds Momma sitting on the sofa in her chocolate-brown pantsuit, making faces at someone who isn't there.

"What's wrong, Momma?"

"What do you mean, wrong?"

"You're making weird faces."

Momma flicks her fingers, like she's killing a fly. "I was just thinkin'."

"About what?"

"You know, that you might like to go on that field trip you've been asking about."

"Really? You're going to let me and Tutor go see the owl?"

Momma gives her a sweet smile. "Actually, I thought you and I could go."

Maddie doesn't trust that sweet smile. Besides, she doesn't want to see the owl with Momma. She wants to see it with Tutor.

Momma pats the sofa beside her. "Come sit by me, Maddie."

"Why?"

"So we can make a plan."

Maddie sits, but not too close. She's seen how Momma uses her sweetness on Daddy when she wants him to do something he doesn't want to do.

Momma slides closer and pats Maddie's leg, with an even prettier smile. "How about you and me go on a little adventure? You know, see that owl and other things. We'll take one of those two-week vacations people talk about."

Maddie's not sure about that. "Won't Daddy come home and wonder where we are?"

"No. He's on a long trip. He'll be gone for quite a while." Momma nudges her arm then winks. "What do you say? Should you and I go have some fun for a change?"

Momma never has fun, so what kind of fun could they have? And what about Tutor? What will he do on Monday if she's not there? Will he think she doesn't want to learn from him anymore? Will he go away and forget all about her? She says, "No. I won't go!"

Momma's smile disappears, and now she looks mad.

Maddie softens her voice to explain, "I can't go, Momma. I have to be here on Monday. You know that."

"Oh, yeah. Him."

"Please, Momma. I have to be here. I just have to."

"Sure, we can be back by then. You betcha. Now go take off that dress and put on those cute bib overalls I ordered for you a while back."

"Those ugly brown overalls? I hate those."

"Do it. And don't forget your toothbrush and comb."

She's worried about what Momma's up to, but she can't help feeling a little excited too. She's waited so long to go outside and see the real world. Still, how can she trust Momma? What if she wants to do something bad while Daddy's away? Something he wouldn't want her doing?

Momma gives her a little push. "Go on. Get packed. I've already got what I need."

Maddie hurries up to her room, finds her blue suitcase, and opens it on the bed. The only time she's used that suitcase was when they went to Littletown to watch Granny die. She realizes what it means. Momma's going to take her to Littletown. She was just waiting for Daddy to be gone on a long trip? That has to be it.

Momma comes in and leans against the door frame, curving her hip in a flirty way like she does with Daddy when she wants her way. "What are you waiting for, honey? Get packed."

Maddie stands her ground. "Momma, I've decided I don't want to see the owl."

"Why's that?"

"You know why! I have to be here on Monday when Tutor comes."

Momma steps closer. "Tutor. Tutor. Tutor. He's really got you under his spell, doesn't he? Well, Maddie girl, I'm going to break that spell. I'm going to set you and myself free at the same time."

That scares Maddie even more. She's right about what Momma wants to do. She looks around the room for help, but there's nothing to help. She needs to call Daddy, right now. Tell him what Momma's doing. Tell him they'll probably be in Littletown by the time he gets home. But she can't call him. Daddy's the one who calls *her*. And there's no way to call Tutor, either. She doesn't know his phone number, or even where he lives. She doesn't know anything about him, except what he told her about his father and his Mum, and what he's taught her, but that's mostly ideas. What will he do when they don't answer the door? Will he go away. Will she ever see him again?

Momma slaps the wall and glares at her. "I told you, get packed! Now quit stalling and do it!"

Maddie doesn't budge. "How can I do it, when I don't know where we're going or what I'm supposed to take? I haven't really ever done this before."

Momma goes to the dresser and yanks out a pair of jeans, a couple of T-shirts, thick cotton socks, all things she bought from a catalog a while back. They're clothes Maddie hates and never wears.

Momma throws the clothes in the suitcase and goes back to the dresser for the brown corduroy overalls that Maddie especially hates. She throws the overalls and a brown, tan, and red plaid flannel shirt on the bed. "Put those on."

Next, she goes to the closet and pushes Maddie's shoes around with her foot, muttering, "That's my girl. Not a practical shoe in the lot." She kicks out a pair of old black patent leather shoes, with scratches on the toes, and scoots them across the floor to Maddie. "These will have to do, until we can get something sturdier."

It's more proof of what Momma plans to do. Why would she need sturdier shoes to go see an owl at the zoo?

Momma snaps, "Don't stand there like you're glued to the floor. Get dressed, get what you need, and come downstairs. The taxi's probably waiting. I'll go see."

Maddie's so upset she can hardly breathe, but she does what Momma said and puts on the plaid shirt and overalls.

She packs her nightgown and underwear, then gets her toothbrush and comb. She stops to think what else she might need.

A dress.

She runs to the closet and gets her white princess dress, her pink and purple unicorn dress, her ballet slippers, and her newer black patent leather shoes. She stuffs everything in the suitcase and carries it downstairs. When she sees two big black suitcases by the door, she wonders how long Momma plans to stay in Littletown. Forever?

While Momma's not looking, she runs to the coat closet and crawls back to Tutor's big box of conceptual glasses. She grabs two pairs, puts them in the pockets of her overalls, and crawls out. As she's sneaking them into her suitcase, the doorbell chimes.

Maddie wills it to be Tutor, but when she opens the door, it's not him. It must be the taxi driver. He comes in, nods to Momma, gets their suitcases, and they all go down in the elevator to the street.

Maddie stands on the sidewalk staring at the bright yellow shine of the taxi, refusing to get in. Momma shoves her into the back seat, and Maddie yells, 'Just wait until Daddy gets home, he's going to be furious when he finds out what you've done! "

Momma gives the driver a little shrug. "Girls. They can be *soo* dramatic." She slams the door, hurries around, and gets in on her own side. The taxi driver slides in behind the steering wheel, and they drive off.

They float through the city streets past men in dark suits and ties with white shirts, like Daddy wears, women in pretty spring dresses, or black slacks, their hair pinned up with a bow. There are Black and Brown people. White people, like her. Teenagers, girls and boys, mostly dressed in shorts or jeans. They laugh and rock back in their chairs at the cafes along the street. People stream along the sidewalks in both directions. Some walking fast past stores with colorful signs. Some stopping to look in the windows. Some already inside, where she'd like to be. Drivers honk their horns from both directions, making her feel like she's caught in a loud chorus of squawking birds. She smiles. Finally, she's outside in the real world. Maybe she'll see Tutor.

When the taxi comes to a stop at a red light, Maddie touches the door handle, daring herself to jump out and disappear into the city so she won't have to go to Littletown. She'll find Tutor. They'll go see the owl at the zoo or wander the city, taking in every sight and sound. Maybe she can stay with Tutor until Daddy comes home from Japan. Then, with Momma gone, they'll finally be free to explore the real world.

Course, it might be scary to be alone in the real world of the city. What if she can't find Tutor? Where would she sleep when it gets dark? She better stay put.

She looks over the front seat of the cab and sees the staring eyes of the driver in the rear view mirror. They're so dark and intense, she can't look away. She squishes herself against the door, but she still sees his eyes. It's like they're trying to tell her something, but she's not sure what it is.

She looks over at Momma. She's mumbling to her clenched hands in her lap. She looks scared. It's not good when Momma looks that scared, but what can *she* do? She can't give her whiskey. Maybe she can help her think about something else.

There's a dog on the street corner that might work. "Look at that cute doggie, Momma. See how happy he is."

Momma won't look, but she has something to say. "City dogs are *not* happy dogs."

Maddie tries again. "That's not true, Momma. Look. That doggie's happy. He's jumping around on his leash with a big smile."

Momma cups her hands around her eyes so she can't see the doggie or anything else.

The driver looks at Maddie, again, like he wants to tell her something that Momma can't know. His eyes look away, but they keep coming back.

Finally, he pulls over to the curb in front of the train station that Maddie remembers from when they went to Littletown to watch Granny die. That has to be where they're going.

Momma gives her arm a nudge. "Get out, Maddie. Let's go."

She holds onto the door handle, but Momma pulls her across the seat, out to the sidewalk, and tells her to stay put. The driver gets their suitcases from the trunk and brings them around. When he hands Maddie her suitcase, she gives him a look that says, *help*. He gives her a quick nod.

Before she can decide if that means he's going to help her, he's back in the taxi and gone. Hopefully, he'll tell Daddy he left them at the train station, so he can come find them in Littletown.

Chapter 18

Momma buys the tickets, pushes Maddie into the last car of the long silver train, then nudges her toward the very back seats. Maddie knows why, it's because Momma wants to sit where she can see everyone, but no one can see her. She doesn't like being seen.

Momma lifts their suitcases onto the overhead shelf and pushes Maddie into the window seat, just as the whistle blows. The train pulls out of the station, rumbling beneath the skyscrapers into the city's dirty back streets where ragged people live in cardboard boxes or beneath blue tarps, their belongings scattered around. Why do they live there? Don't they have a nice house or a condo to go back to?

Maybe not. Tutor said *he* lived on the streets after he'd learned everything from the books in the library. Maybe he lived in a cardboard box. If he did, it must have been cold at night. And scary. She wouldn't care if it was scary; she'd stay in a cardboard box if Tutor was there. She'd do anything if Tutor was there.

When the train moves out of the city, she presses her nose against the glass and looks back at the shrinking skyline. It's like everything she's ever known is being pulled away, leaving nothing but a sad lonely girl in ugly bib overalls and old black shoes. Where's the real Maddie? Will she ever be back?

She yanks at the straps of her overalls, wondering what Mim would think of them. She'd probably agree they're dumb. She's going to need Mim so bad now that Tutor's gone. Will she be able to find her in the country? Or will she be one those absent things that you long for, but they're not really there?

If only she'd been brave enough to jump out of the taxi when she thought about doing it. She and Tutor could be exploring the city right now. She'll probably never see Tutor again, and she might never see Daddy, either. Oh no. She has to see Daddy.

She glares at Momma and pushes her arm. Momma doesn't notice. She's too busy hiding her face in her cream-colored cashmere scarf, sipping her whiskey. Her long, chocolate-brown pantsuit legs are crossed, trapping Maddie in. If Momma falls asleep, she won't be able to go to the bathroom. She'd have to fly over the seats. But if she could fly, she wouldn't waste it on going to the bathroom, she'd soar straight out the door or an open window. Too bad the train's going so fast. She might get hurt.

She concentrates on the warmth of the sunlight sinking into the brown corduroy of her overalls. It reminds her of being on the condo balcony, warming her legs in the morning sun while she watched the high-rise window washers on the building next door. She won't be doing that anymore.

She sees a glint of light moving along the rails of the parallel tracks and thinks of sliver of silver light that took Tutor's Mum away. Maybe *this* silver light will turn *her* into a silver bird, and she can fly away. She squints at the light willing it to happen.

It doesn't happen. She's still sitting on the back seat of the train next to Momma.

She yanks at the straps of her overalls again. Why did Momma make her wear these stupid things? Does Momma want her to be some farm girl, out gathering eggs from mean chickens every day?

No. The chickens aren't mean. They're just mothers trying to save their baby chicks. Is Momma trying to save her baby chick by taking her to Littletown? No, Momma's trying to save herself.

Maddie tries to focus on something happy. The happiest day of her life was when Tutor came and Daddy told him not to forget her imagination. Tutor didn't forget. He made her laugh with his magic sparkles and helped her see the world in different ways through his conceptual sunglasses. Luckily, she remembered to bring some of those glasses with her, but will they work in the country without Tutor?

By now, Tutor's so far away, he's almost unreal. Like he's from a dream she once had, or a story she read in a book, or made up in her mind. Will that happen to Daddy too? Will he fade into nothing but a story? No. Daddy's too real. He's been there her whole life. Besides, won't lose Daddy. He'll keep looking for her until he finds her, no matter how long it takes. She clings to that thought, willing herself to believe it's true.

There's no sign of the city now. All she sees are trees and green or yellow pastures flying by, with a few cows and horses standing around. She takes a deep breath, trying to make sense of how it feels. She's spent so long dreaming of the real world, and now she's finally in it. But it's nothing like she imagined. She's not free, she's just in a different kind of cage, a moving cage with Momma in charge. Momma can take her anywhere she wants. Who's going to stop her?

Daddy will. He has to.

Somewhere in the train, a baby cries. It reminds Maddie of the lost baby she needs to find. Will she be able to do that without Tutor? Or will she have to go her whole life not knowing if the baby is real? She can't stand that idea. She has to know.

Maybe Momma will tell her the truth, now that she's got what she wants, and they're on their way to Littletown.

She nudges Momma's arm. "Can I ask you something, Momma."

Momma opens one eye "What?"

"Um…I was wondering. Was there ever a baby boy?"

Momma's other eye flies open. "What do you mean? Who told you that?"

"Nobody, told me. I just thought I heard a baby cry one time."

"Well, you're mistaken." Momma pulls her cashmere scarf up to her chin.

"But I think I *saw* him too."

Momma wags her head like she's hearing nonsense. She drinks more whiskey and won't answer.

"Please, Momma. I need to know."

"I told you. There–was–no–baby!"

Maddie's not about to give up. "But I'm pretty sure I saw him. And sometimes, I hear him cry in my dream."

"Well, that tells you what it is. A dream."

"No, Momma, it's not a dream! I heard him for real when I was little."

Momma silences her with a mean look and straightens up. She uncrosses her long brown pantsuit legs and quickly crosses them the other way, still trapping Maddie in. "I'm telling you. There's no boy." She slinks down into her scarf and closes her eyes.

Maddie presses her nose against the window and watches a row of tall trees fly by. They must be those poplar trees she's read about. She loves those trees. She'd love to climb to the top of a poplar tree in a blowing wind with the sunset burning fiery red. She'd feel safe up there, held in by the tight upward-facing branches, up where she knows she belongs. White Bird would come and they'd fly across the sky together and find Tutor.

The rumble of the train makes her sad. It's like a low moan that won't stop. Like the moan she feels inside her, trying to get out. But still, she's out in the real world. She should try to see it.

They leave the poplar trees behind, gliding past a golden field where towering bales of yellow straw cast long shadows in the morning sun. The scene is beautiful, like a painting from Daddy's book of Great American Artists. She imagines climbing on top one of those bales, rolling across the countryside on wild ride. She'd end up in Neverland. Tutor would come, and they'd stay there forever, doing fun things.

She slaps her leg. "No! I don't believe in fairytales anymore. I believe in real things, like Tutor, and birds, and trains. I don't want to be a fairytale princess. I don't want to be *Snow White*, or *Alice in Wonderland*. I want to live with real people, in the real world. I want to see real owls, travel to Japan, where I'd ride the escalators all night with the cats of Enoshima Island. I want to find out what the whispering Buddha says."

As the train rumbles on, she thinks of something bad that she hadn't thought of before. What will she do if Tutor's not around to teach her new things? And if Daddy's not there, and she doesn't have any books. How will she learn anything about anything? And, how's she going to keep from dying of boredom? She could have at least brought one or two books. Maybe Daddy's *Audubon Book of Country Birds*. She might need a book like that. And she might need a book of maps, so she can see where to go if it turns out Daddy can't find her. She might need books about all kinds of things in the country, but she doesn't have a single one.

She looks over at Momma. She's still hiding down in her scarf. If she'd go to sleep, maybe Maddie could escape. She could turn into a bird and fly down the aisle to the door and fly straight out next time the train stops. Then she wouldn't need books. She could find her own lessons and have something to teach Daddy and Tutor next time she sees them. If she ever does.

The train whistles and shrieks to a stop. Momma jerks awake and pushes her scarf down from her face where it's supposed to be. She stands, jerks the suitcases from the shelf, gives Maddie her suitcase to carry, and nudges her up the aisle to the door.

They're the only ones that get off the train, and Maddie sees why. It's just an old worn out station with a rickety wood platform on each side of the tracks. There's no one around. It doesn't look like anyone's been here in a very long time.

The train rumbles away and disappears into a sliver of silver light. Now she's alone with Momma in complete silence. That kind silence that makes her want to cover her ears and cry.

Momma giggles. She's been drinking whiskey the whole time on the train, and now she's trying to sit on top of one of her suitcases, but she's tipsy. She stands, giggles, tries again, and fails. She slaps her thigh. "Boy, am I glad I'm here."

Maddie scoffs. "Here? There's nothing here except empty grass fields and those blue mountains way over there along the horizon."

Momma gets a dreamy look in her eyes. "Oh, yes. The Blue Mountains. I met your Daddy in the Blue Mountain Hot Springs. Full moon night, steam rising up from the water where the cold river water mixes with the hot water of the springs, stars twinkling all around. It was magic, pure magic."

"I've never heard about that before."

Momma jerks back from her dreamy look. "What? What did I say?"

"You said you met Daddy at the Blue Mountain Hot Springs. You said it was magic."

"I didn't say that."

"Yes, you did. I heard you."

Momma shakes her head, trying to deny it, but Maddie knows what she heard.

Momma looks all around, with a big frown on her face. "Damn. Where is she?"

"Where's who, Momma?"

"Star. She said she'd meet us here. Where in the hell is she?"

"Who's Star?"

"My friend."

"If she's your friend, how come I don't know her?"

Momma won't answer, instead she says, "Come on. We need to get away from the tracks. Quick. Before another train comes."

Momma drags her suitcases down the rough wooden steps and across the train tracks to the other side where there's a dirt road heading off through the tall grass fields.

Maddie carries her suitcase across the tracks, and drags it on down the road over the rocks, trying to catch up. She yells, "Where are we going, Momma?"

Momma calls back. "I don't know. Hopefully, Star will come and tell us."

Maddie frowns. "Star knows where we're going, but you don't?"

"Well, damn, I hope she does."

Momma hurries along the road, trying to stay balanced in her high-heeled shoes.

Maddie tries to catch up, but the wheels on her suitcase are too little. They keep getting stuck in the rocks and ruts. If Momma doesn't care about that, why did she make her come all this way in the first place? She could go faster if she was alone. Then they'd both be happy.

Momma stops and lets out a hoot and Maddie finally catches up.

Momma yells, "There she is. See that pink Cadillac convertible. That's her. That's Star's car. She's had it forever."

The Cadillac screams down the road and slides to a stop in a high cloud of dust and flying gravel. When the dust settles Maddie sees what it is. A beautiful pink convertible car, with a big silver bird on the front of the hood. Does that mean the car can fly?

Star jumps out of the car, waving her arms. "I'm sorry. I'm sorry. I fell asleep out by the swimming pool. I should've set an alarm."

Maddie has never seen anyone like Star, not even on TV. She's as tall as Daddy, with strong tanned arms, long blond hair, and shiny pink lipstick that matches her car, perfectly She's wearing a tiny red bikini, a gold chain around her neck, a sparkling gold ring on her right hand, with a diamond.

As they hug, Star flashes Maddie a knowing smile over her shoulder. "So, this is our Maddie, huh? She sure looks like a regular farm girl in those overalls. Perfect. Nobody will suspect a thing."

Star drops her hug with Momma and sweeps Maddie up in her arms. She twirls her around and around, making her legs fly, and squeezing her chest so tight, she can hardly breathe. Maddie squeaks, "Stop it, Star."

Star twirls her one more time and sets her down.

Momma shakes her head at Star. "Well? Are we ready? Should we go?"

Star nods. "Right. Right. We should get out of here. By the way, I've found a place."

Momma gives her a sideways look. "I hope it's good."

Star gives her a thumbs-up. "Oh yes, it's good. It's perfect." She opens the trunk of the Cadillac and puts the suitcases inside.

Momma opens the door for Maddie to get in back, then she gets in front next to Star.

Star starts the engine, and they take off, speeding down a country road in a pink convertible Cadillac to somewhere Momma doesn't know, and Star says is perfect. Maybe they're not going to Littletown.

Chapter 19

Maddie slides to the middle of the back seat. How in the world did she end up in a pink Cadillac convertible, in the middle of nowhere, with someone as big and beautiful as Star. It's like someone cast a spell and the whole world changed. Was it the magician Tutor?

She sinks into the smooth, warm silkiness of the black leather seat. If only she were wearing her pink-and-purple unicorn dress. It would look perfect against the smooth shine of the black leather and the hot pink of Star's car. If Tutor were beside her in his black magician suit and shimmering white shirt, it would be even better. She wouldn't be so worried about where they're going. But Tutor isn't here, and he doesn't know where she is, so he won't be coming to save her, even if he did say he'd always watch over her.

Star reaches over and squeezes Momma's shoulder. "I'm so glad you're here, Darlin'. I've missed you."

Momma moans. "I didn't think I'd make it, Star. I thought I'd hurt myself before I could get free."

"Please, Sweetie. Don't talk like that."

Did Momma just say she'd hurt herself? Maddie knows Momma's been sad, but she didn't think she was sad enough to do that. She must have really been missing Star. Maddie understands that kind of missing. She's feeling it right now. Momma's got Star, but she doesn't have anyone now that Tutor's gone. Maybe forever. It's so unfair.

Star's big blue eyes meet Maddie's in the rearview mirror. "I've missed you too, Maddie. You're a lot bigger than the last time I saw you, but still lean as a bean."

That's a surprise. Where did Star see her before?

Momma glances back from the front seat, then smirks at Star. "Yeah, she's a lot bigger and a lot smarter. Kind of big in the britches, if you ask me, but she's my girl, and I love her."

If Momma loves her, why did she call her 'big in the britches'? That's mean. And why did she take her away from Tutor, Daddy, and the city? Everything she's ever known? That doesn't feel like love.

Star looks at Momma and chuckles. "Mouse is still here."

"Really?" Momma says, raising an eyebrow. "I figured she'd be long gone by now. She hated Littletown, always said she sure as hell wasn't going to marry a farm boy. *Did she marry a farm boy?*"

"Nah, she's still single. Always will be, I guess. The question is, why didn't *you* marry a farm boy? You could have had any Tom, Dick, or Harry you wanted, what with your gorgeous *figur* and *nat-chu-ral* blond hair. Me, I get my blond from a bottle." Star fluffs her hair sending it streaming over the front seat.

Momma, laughs. "Oh, yeah, *Harry*. That would have been a nightmare."

Star hoots. "I thought you liked pigs."

"Pigs are okay, but who wants to wallow around in the mud your whole life? I prefer steeds."

Star hoots again. "Oh, you mean Tom. Now that would have been a match made in heaven. You should have married Tom."

Momma glances back at Maddie. "Maybe we shouldn't be talking like this."

Momma's right. They shouldn't be talking like she isn't sitting right there, wondering how they can joke about Momma marrying someone besides Daddy."

Star meets her eyes in the mirror again. "We're just kiddin', Maddie. Having some girl talk. We haven't seen each other in ages." She glances at Momma. "How long has it been?"

Momma shrugs. "Three, maybe four years."

Maddie leans between the front seats. "Is that when you saw me, Star? When I was four, when Granny died?"

"No, not then. I was in California at the time Granny died. It was when–"

Momma shoots Star a look that says keep quiet.

They rattle along the dirt road in silence, until Star slows the car and comes to a stop. Maddie stands up and sees another old road, going left and right.

Star turns left.

There's still nothing for Maddie to see. No buildings. No cars. Not even a tree. The only thing besides the endless grass fields are those blue mountains way off in the distance. The mountains where Momma met Daddy in the Blue Mountain Hot Springs. She'd love to see those hot springs and sit in the warm steaming water.

Momma gives her a mean look. "Sit down, Maddie!"

Her words feel like a slap. Why can't Momma say things in a nice way? She smiles and laughs with Star, but always gives Maddie her mean side. Why can't she ever have the nice side of Momma?

She sits down and focuses on the car rattling over the lumpy grass and weeds growing through cracked pavement. This road can't have been used in a long time, so why are they driving on it?

Star and Momma aren't talking now, which gives Maddie time to think about what they've already said. Who's Mouse and why does she have such a funny name? Is it a real name? Does she look like a mouse? And who are Tom, Dick, and Harry? It sounds like they were boys in Momma's high school that she could have married, instead of Daddy. But maybe that's not true. Maybe Star *was* just kidding around. Besides, didn't Momma get all dreamy-eyed when she thought about meeting Daddy in the hot springs. Does Star know about that?

Maddie leans forward to ask, "Star, did you know Momma and Daddy when they met at the hot springs?"

Star's eyes light up in the mirror. "Sure, I did." She gives Momma's leg a quick squeeze. "Blue Mountain Lodge. Right? That was quite a night, if I remember correctly."

Momma says, "I don't want to talk about Blue Mountain Lodge. It's the past. The past is gone. There's no way back."

Maddie yells, "No, Momma! No! We can't leave Daddy in the past. I love him."

Star tilts her head toward Momma. "She's got a point."

Momma hisses. "That's too damn bad! I'm not living in that city anymore, and I'm not losing Maddie. I can't go through that again, Star. You know, I can't."

"I know, honey."

There are tears in Momma's voice, but so what? They can't leave Daddy in the past. It's too terrible to even think about. "Momma, why do you want to leave Daddy behind? He doesn't deserve that."

Momma growls, "He put me in a cage!"

"No! He didn't! You put yourself in the cage by being scared all the time! And you put me in the same cage."

Momma yells, "Shut up, Maddie! Just shut up!"

Everyone's upset now. Maddie knows it's her fault, but she doesn't care. She has to be with Daddy, no matter what Momma says. How can she live without him? And without Tutor. She just can't. It's not fair.

They're still flying over the bumpy road in the Cadillac, but the fun's all gone. Maddie needs something to help her escape her sad thoughts. But what? There's nothing out here.

Finally, she sees something rising out of the grass. As they get closer, she realizes it's a tower with wires running between other towers. They must be the lines that carry electricity from one city to the next. High tension power towers is what Daddy called them. Does that mean there's a city nearby? A place she can go and get help to find him, if he can't find her?

They leave the towers behind, and soon, Maddie spots something ahead. It's a building, with red, round-topped things out front, a poplar tree in the back, and tall green grass all around.

Star pulls in next to the building and says, "Okay. This is it."

Momma looks shocked. "You're kidding me, right? An old gas station?"

"Nope. Not kidding. It's the perfect place. Clearly, no one ever comes out here. It's been for sale for a long time, so the owner is happy to get a little rent. The utilities were left on for potential buyers, so you'll have that."

Star jumps out. She gets the suitcases from the trunk, takes them inside. She comes back and lifts Maddie over the side of the Cadillac without opening the door. She sets her down and takes her hand, making her feel like a little kid. "Come on, girl. Let's go see your new digs."

Momma stays in the car, looking disgusted. But it's her own fault. She's the one that wanted to leave Daddy.

Maddie follows Star inside the gas station. There's nothing there except rows of empty shelves. No snacks or soda pop, like she thought there might be.

Star leads her to a tall cabinet with a glass door. "This is your refrigerator. Can you believe it still works? See there, I bought you some things."

Maddie sees orange juice and milk, jam, Pop Tarts, pickles, and other stuff that mostly looks like breakfast food. What are they going to eat for lunch and dinner?

Star points to a nearby shelf. "And these are your dry goods: bread, cereal, crackers. Stuff like that."

Maddie tries to look happy, but she's not. If Tutor were here, it would be an adventure. One of those field trips they talked about, to go see the owl and other things. But wait. Didn't Momma say they were going to see an owl. She hasn't seen an owl. Where is it?

Star goes out and drags Momma inside, saying, "Come on, Darlin'. Believe me it's the perfect place for someone that doesn't want to be found. It's only for a short time. Then we'll find you your own place and you can get settled in. It's perfect."

So, it's true. Momma does plan to stay. But this doesn't seem like Littletown.

Star pulls Momma towards a door at the back of the main room. "Come on. I'll show you the living space. It's quite cute. There's a closet and an old dresser they left, and I got you a bed, but you're gonna have to sleep together."

Momma groans. "Really, Star?"

"It's the best I could do in three days. You should've given me more notice if you wanted a castle with room service."

They go into the room, where Maddie sees that the so-called *bed* is nothing but a thin mattress on the floor, covered with a thick, blue-and-white-checked quilt. Maddie tries to imagine sleeping there next to Momma. Will they both fit?

It looks like Momma has the same question. She stares at the bed, shaking her head. "Oh, Star. This isn't going to work."

Star drapes her arm around Momma's shoulder. "Sure it is. You've just got to think of what it gets you. You're back in the country. You're home. You're free. That's what you wanted. Right?"

Momma pulls her fingers through her hair, and tries to smile. "You're right, at least, I won't be in the city."

Star takes them to a bathroom where there's a toilet, a sink, and a metal cabinet. She points to the cabinet. "You'll find towels and a couple of washcloths in there, but I'm afraid you'll have to take bird baths in the sink. As you can see, there's no shower or tub."

Maddie knows that's not good There's nothing Momma loves more than soaking in a big bathtub with her whiskey. Besides, how can they take a bath in a sink? They're not birds.

They go outside through a back door in the bedroom and Star points up at a platform at the side of the station. "That's your water tank up there. I don't think the pump works, but it's high enough, it still feeds. You shouldn't run out of water. I climbed up there and it's quite full. So, you have that."

Star closes one eye and stares up at the sky like she's trying to remember what else she needs to say. "Oh. I know. I wouldn't turn on the outside lights at night. The road's barely used, but you don't want some night wanderer stopping in for a visit. Some cowboy or drifter. Just stay in the back room with the front lights turned off. You'll be fine. I'll be back in a few days to bring you more food and any news I get. I'm sorry there's no phone service out here. You'll have to rely on me."

Momma stares at the floor, shaking her head in frustration. "Did you at least think to bring me some whiskey."

Star thumps her forehead. "Oh, no. I'm sorry. I should have thought of that. Next time. Okay? I've got to go now."

Star pulls them into a quick hug, spins on her pink heels, and heads out to her Cadillac. They follow her and stand outside by the door. With a wave of her hand, she's back in her car, speeding down the road in a cloud of dust, leaving them behind in an old gas station in the middle of nowhere.

Chapter 20

Maddie stands next to Momma watching the dust swirling up from Star's Cadillac. When the car and the dust disappear, they go back inside. Momma stares at Maddie looking lost, then shakes herself and shrugs. "Okay. I guess I'll go change."

Maddie follows her to the bedroom and watches as she changes out of her chocolate brown pantsuit into a pair of black Levi jeans and a bright white shirt, like Daddy wears. She pulls on shiny black boots, cinches her waist with a sparkly belt studded with hot pink rhinestones, and twirls around, showing off every side. "There. That's better. Now I feel like myself."

Maddie is amazed. What happened to Momma? She's transformed into a pretty country cowgirl. Did a fairy godmother sneak in and wave her magic wand? "You're beautiful, Momma. You look like a rodeo queen."

"Why, thank you, ma'am." Momma gives her a bow, then glances around. "Now, where did I put my horse."

Maddie giggles. "It wouldn't be in here. It'd be out in the barn, if we had a barn." She wishes she had pretty cowgirl clothes instead of the ugly brown overalls she's been stuck in all day. She does have those dresses she sneaked into her suitcase, but this isn't the kind of place for a dress. Besides, she doesn't want Momma to know she brought them. She might get mad.

Momma's eyes flash green. She smiles and pats her hip like she's got a cowboy's gun in her holster. "Well, pardner, we may as well look around. I sure hope Star left us some coffee."

"There might be some. Follow me." Maddie leads her out to the shelf where Star put what she called the dry food.

Momma picks up a jar and frowns. "Really, Star? Dried crystal coffee. I can't drink this crap."

Maddie points to the cold stuff on the refrigerated shelves. "At least there's some orange juice and milk. I wonder if she left any cookies?"

"Who knows what she left. We better make a list of things for next time she comes."

"Where does Star live, Momma?"

"In Littletown. We went to high school together."

"Are *we* in Littletown now?"

"No."

Maddie can't tell from her face if she's lying. "But I thought that's where we were going, Momma."

"I didn't say that."

"So where are we?"

She flaps her hand in Maddie's face. "Never mind that." She puts on a smile and starts pushing through the cold stuff. "Let's see if we can find some vittles. I'm starving."

"Vittles?"

"You know, lunch."

Maddie finds a package of hot dogs behind the milk. "We could have these, if there's any way to cook them."

"I can't imagine there is, but why don't you look around."

Maddie slips and slides through the aisles between the empty shelves. When she gets to the side wall, she spots one of those machines that cook hot dogs on heated rods, like Moe has in *The Simpsons*. She yells, "Come see what I found, Momma!"

Momma comes and flips the switch, and the metal rods start to spin. "Will you look at that, Maddie. This place must have been open more recently than it looks. Star did good. We'll have to thank her."

Maddie feels the power in Momma's words. She never says "we," never talks like she wants to do things together. Back at the condo, she always had to be in charge, alone.

She stares at this new version of Momma, her shiny blond hair, that little smile on her lips that makes her seem soft and nice, like someone you might be able to talk to and have fun with.

Momma flicks her hand in Maddie's face and turns away like she doesn't like being looked at that close. "Let's see. Where's the bread? Go grab that and see if Star left us any mustard. I saw a picnic table out back where we can eat. Is that okay with you? "

There. It happened again. Momma asked for her opinion. "It's okay with me, Momma. I think I saw some pickles. Should we have those with our hot dogs?"

"Sure," Momma says. "Pickles are good. Get those and some paper plates. "

Maddie runs to get everything and comes back with her arms full.

Momma places a hot dog and a pickle on two plates, and says, "Come on, grab the bread. Let's go."

Maddie can hardly believe it. They really are partners. Not only that, but she's going to have a hot dog picnic with Momma on a real picnic table for the first time in her life.

This is starting to be fun.

They go out the back door from the bedroom, cut across the grass to the picnic table. Momma sits on one side and Maddie on the other. Neither of them says a word as they eat their hot dogs and pickles, without mustard. It's a funny lunch, but it tastes good, and they're having fun.

Maddie opens her eyes wide and shoves her hot dog into her mouth like she's about to take a huge bite. Momma crosses her eyes and moves her mouth in a funny way, like a cow chewing its cud. Maddie laughs and chokes on her last bite. Momma snaps, "Don't mess around, Maddie. We don't need any disasters out here. There's no one to help us."

There's that old mean Momma again, just when they were having fun. Or did she make the whole thing up? The way she changes so fast, it hurts, and it's confusing. She can't tell if Momma likes or hates her. She never has trouble knowing how Tutor feels. He's nice, he's funny, and he's smart. Tutor's her friend, her blood brother. If that's true, will he come rescue her like a real brother would?

Momma's face softens. "You know, we don't need that electric cooker, we can cook our hot dogs out here from now on. See that fire pit by the rock wall. We can sit cross-legged on the ground, find some willows for roasting sticks, and eat like we're camping. For dessert, we can put roasted marshmallows on Graham Crackers with chocolate and have s'mores. Matter of fact, we should put s'mores ingredients on our list for Star. You know about s'mores, right?"

"Um...sounds like roasted marshmallows and chocolate on Graham Crackers. Right?"

"Right, smarty pants. They're really good."

Did she say, *smarty pants*? Does that mean Momma thinks she's smart. That's nice, but she needs to stay on her guard. Momma could change into her mean self at any moment.

Momma reaches across the table and gives her hand a quick squeeze. "Here's one for you, Maddie. Why did the chicken cross the road?"

Maddie knows the answer, but she shrugs, so she can hear Momma say it.

"To get to the other side, silly."

"I knew that."

Momma's eyes move back and forth like she's thinking of another one. "Okay. What do you do when a cow eats too much hay and gets bloated."

Maddie *doesn't* know the answer to this one, so she shrugs again.

Momma thrusts her hand out quick like she's got a knife. "You stab it in the side so the gas can get out."

Maddie gasps. "Doesn't that kill the cow?"

"No. That's what you have to do to save it."

"But it's so mean."

Momma catches her eyes. "Listen, Maddie. You do what you have to do out here in the country. That's your first lesson. You're a country girl now."

Is it true? Will she be a country girl from now on? "I don't know how to be a country girl, Momma. Are you going to teach me?"

"Sure. You like to learn things, don't you?"

Momma's never taught her anything, except what not to do. Will she finally learn something else? Things she didn't learn from her books or from Tutor and Daddy? Will Momma teach her how the country world works?

Momma chomps down her last bite of hot dog, smacks her lips, and stands up. "Come on, pardner. Let's go for a wander."

Momma heads off through the tall green grass, patting the pretend gun on her hip. Every now and then, she takes it out to aim at an imaginary deer, or rabbit.

Maddie runs to catch up. She loves this funny version of Momma. She's so fun. "Momma, how come you're so good at walking fast through the grass when you've never done it?"

Momma glances back at her. "What do you mean, never done it?"

"I mean, the only place we ever walk at the condo is in the living room, the kitchen, and up and down the stairs. It feels strange to have my feet on real ground."

"Well, I had a life before the condo, didn't I? Walking through grass is like riding a horse, you never forget how to do it."

Maddie wails. "But I never learned how to do it. I never learned how to do anything, except read. You know that, Momma."

Momma takes hands. "I'm sorry, honey. I'm sorry. It's just that–" Maddie sees a shimmer of tears in Momma's eyes, and it looks like she wants to say something nice. Instead, she heads off through the grass even faster. Why is it so hard for Momma to talk to her?

Maddie can hardly see through her own tears, but she doesn't want to be left behind. She hurries through the grass as fast as she can. "Wait, Momma. The grass is too tall for me. I can't go that fast."

Momma waits for her to catch up, and they move forward together, pushing the tall grass aside with their knees. Momma starts singing an old country song.

Maddie joins in. They sing the whole song as a soft breeze ripples through the grass, scattering sparks of gold light across the field, almost as if Tutor was there, shaking his sleeves.

She misses Tutor, so much. There are things she wants to show him in the country, questions she wants to ask. And how wonderful it would be if he could meet this nice version of Momma. Maybe she would like him, and he'd like her, and they could all be friends.

But right now, she can't think about Tutor. She needs to keep her mind on this moment with Momma, so she can learn how to see in a country way.

Maybe Momma will teach her. Or maybe tomorrow, she'll be the same mean ol' Momma she's always been.

Chapter 21

Maddie sits with Momma on the wall, clacking their heels against the rocks as the evening sky burns orange and red over the distant Blue Mountains. She wants to ask Momma about meeting Daddy at the hot springs again, but she's afraid it would break the spell of the magic.

When the sun shoots a last blaze of gold light across the grass fields and sinks into the blue haze of the mountains, Maddie realizes she's about to spend a night with Momma in in a completely new place.

As the sky darkens, the stars begin to appear. When Orion is completely drawn, Maddie points him out to Momma. "See, that constellation? That's Orion. He's the son of the sea god, Poseidon."

"Is that right?" Momma points out a few constellations of her own, "There's Scorpius and Pisces, you know, Pisces, those two fishes tied together at the tail?" She jumps off the wall, and says, "Come with me, I've got a surprise for you."

"Really? A surprise? Oh boy!"

They run inside. Momma grabs something from her suitcase and heads for the bathroom, saying, "I'll be back in a jiffy."

While she waits, Maddie leans back against the wall and looks at the room. There's not much to see, just an old dresser and a closet without its sliding doors. There's one small window set high above the narrow mattress on the floor. She could never get out that window, if there was a fire or if a bad man came in the night. Unless there's a chair. No. There's no chair and no rug on the rough wooden planks of the floor. No pictures or curtains, just blank walls with peeling white paint, like you'd find in the orphanage of a Charles Dickens's story. There's a bare light bulb hanging from the ceiling on a wire. It's too bright and casts dark, spooky shadows in the closet, that look like something might be hiding in there.

Momma comes back from the bathroom, looking happy, like she's just had some whiskey. Will she be mean?

Maddie doesn't wait to find out. She goes to take *her* turn in the bathroom. She sits on the old, cracked toilet seat under the flickering fluorescent lights and stares at the crooked gray metal door that doesn't quite fit its frame. What if the door gets stuck and she can't get out? Will Momma save her? Or will she be stuck in the bathroom until Daddy comes, if he ever does?

She hurries back to Momma and finds her slinking around the bedroom in a pair of blue silk pajamas. She sees Maddie, and throws something her way.

Maddie gasps when she opens the package and sees her own pair of blue silk pajamas. "They're beautiful, Momma. We can be twins."

Momma gives her a little shimmy. "Put 'em on, why don'tcha."

Maddie undresses, slowly, feeling self-conscious. Momma never watches her dress or undress. She never watches her do much of anything. But don't think about that.

The silky softness of the pajamas feels wonderful on her skin after wearing rough corduroy all day. She hugs herself and gives Momma a little shimmy. They grab hands and spin around the room, laughing and bumping into the walls. Maddie can't believe it. It's almost as fun as being with Tutor. Is it real, or did she fall into a dream?

Momma trips on the corner of the mattress and sprawls across the floor. She scrambles to her feet and scowls down at the mattress. "Damn it, Star! What were you thinking? I can't sleep on that. I need a drink."

She hurries to her suitcase and comes back trying to hide her bottle. She lies down on the mattress and pulls the blue-and white-checked quilt up to her nose. The quilt pokes up, and Maddie knows she's taking a drink. Why did she tell Star to bring whiskey, if she already had some?

It's not fair for Momma to drink whiskey right now, when they were having such fun. It only lasted a minute, and now Happy Momma's gone.

Maddie stares down at the narrow bed, wondering if it's safe to get in. What if Momma gets so drunk she rolls on top of her and she can't breathe? Or what if she can't sleep because she's never slept with anyone before? How long will that make the night last?

Momma opens one eye and squints at her. "Whatcha lookin' at. Turn the light off and get in bed."

When she flips off the switch, bright moonlight pours in through the small window above the mattress. She hadn't noticed the moon was so full. Now, its pearly white glow shines across the mattress and part of Momma's face. On that side she looks like an angel, but the other side is hidden in dark shadow. The light and shadow make her seem like a person who can't decide who she is, and that's exactly how she acts, swinging between nice and mean so fast Maddie never knows what she'll get.

Maddie can't think about that. It's been a long day, and she needs to see if she can sleep. She kneels down on the mattress, but she's not sure what to do. Should she sleep on her back so her knees don't bump Momma, or maybe curl up on her side, real close to her edge of the bed. She tries it, but the mattress is so narrow, her bottom touches Momma's arm. It tightens and pulls away.

Maddie rolls onto her back and holds her arms against her sides. She looks over at Momma. Even in the moonlight, she can see Momma clutching the whiskey bottle like a baby refusing to give up its bottle. The sight of that brings back her frustration about the missing baby. Without Tutor's help, how will she ever find out if he's real? Momma's not going to tell her anything. Why can't she at least know who the baby belongs to? Is it Momma's baby? Is it Star's?

She wants to ask, but she knows Momma doesn't need any hard questions right now. She needs to wear her pretty cowgirl clothes and blue silk pajamas so that she can feel like her old self and not be afraid of whatever she's afraid of in the city.

Maddie tries to sleep, but there's another question she just has to ask Momma. She rolls onto her side and presses her forehead against Momma's arm, hoping she's awake.

She hears a puff of air, and Momma says. "What's wrong."

"I need to know something, Momma."

"What?"

"You're taking us away from Daddy, but I don't know why. I need to know. Did you stop loving him?"

Momma moans. "It's not that simple."

"But I love Daddy. Don't you?"

Momma jerks the quilt up and takes another drink.

Maddie pulls the quilt down. "Please, Momma. I have to know what happened. Why do you want to leave him in the past?"

Momma moans again. "It's not him. It's me, Maddie. I can't live in the city anymore."

Maddie tries to understand. "But why? Is it because you miss Star too much?"

She nods. "Yes. Yes. That's it. I miss Star."

"But why can't she come to the city, sometimes. Or we can come and see her in Littletown. Then we can go home and be with Daddy. Why can't we do both things?"

"We just can't, Maddie! Now go to sleep!" She takes another drink of whiskey and rolls onto her side.

Maddie pulls the quilt over her head so she can cry. It's not fair for Momma to leave Daddy. She doesn't have a good reason, so how can it be so important? Why can't Momma ever tell her the truth about anything?

She pushes the quilt off her face and stares up into the cold white loneliness of the full moon night. She closes her eyes, but the moonlight comes through her lids, like the sweet scent of Tutor's hair when she put his hat over her face after Momma sent him away. His scent was so strong, she could almost see him. His little black beard, shiny turquoise eyes, and silly wiggles. His sparkles and smiles that always made her laugh. Remembering all that, she can almost see him.

She hears a sound from out back and holds her breath, waiting for it to come again.

It does. It's an owl. "Who-hoo! Who-hoo! Who-hoo!"

Is it a message from Tutor? Did he send Owl to tell her he's on his way? She needs to go outside and see.

She gets to her feet, grabs her shoes, and tiptoes across the room and out the back door without waking Momma.

The haunting sound of the owl comes again: "Who-hoo! Who-hoo! Who-hoo!

Maddie Who-hoos back and whispers, "It's me, Owl. It's Maddie. I'm here. Where are you?"

Owl hoots back from the high branches of the poplar tree. She can't see him, but she knows he's up there waiting.

She's never climbed a tree before, but she should be able to do it. Why not? Anyone can climb a tree. Besides, Tutor said everything you learn gives you a new way of seeing the world. Like when they saw through the eyes of a red-eyed tree frog. Maybe she can climb the poplar tree like a red-eyed tree frog.

She crawls into the lower limbs. The tight branches hold onto her like they're afraid she'll go too high and fall. As if the tree is trying to protect her. "Let me go, tree. I need to see Owl. I need to ask him if he's seen Tutor."

She grips a higher branch and pulls. The tree moans and lets her go.

One branch at a time, she climbs until she's high above the ground. She needs to go higher. She leans back and tries to see Owl up in the top branches. The moon's too bright, but maybe that's his silhouette.

He hoots again. "Don't be afraid, Maddie. Come on up and be here with me."

It's scary to be so high, but she feels braver than she's ever felt in her life. She's climbing a tree, and that's all that matters.

A breeze rocks the tree. Will it fling her out into the night? Will Owl help her fly?

A cold hard wind hits her face and flips the tree violently back and forth. She holds tight and gasps for air.

"Not yet, Wind. It's not time to go flying. I've got to get up to Owl."

Owl cries out with his same words. "Who-hoo! Who-hoo!"

"I hear you, Owl. Wait for me. I'm almost there."

When she finally gets high enough to see him straight on, Owl looks her with his big, bright yellow eyes. He blinks and turns his head all the way around, showing her what she's always wanted to see. He's not afraid at all, and neither is she. They're both right where they want to be, in a high place above the world, on a full-moon night, with no one to tell them what to do.

Owl tips his head in a way that looks just like Tutor. She's about to ask where Tutor is when she hears a shriek from below.

She stretches out from the tree and sees Momma below, running in circles, screaming and flapping her hands like a frantic chicken that wants to peck somebody's legs. What's wrong with her?

Owl looks at Maddie like he's disappointed. He blinks, sighs, and takes flight.

Maddie whispers, "Please, Owl, tell Tutor I'm here. Tell Daddy too. They need to come save me."

Owl circles the tree, showing he understands. Then, with a whoosh of his wings, he disappears into the darkness beyond the water tower.

Owl's gone, but Maddie still wants to be in the tree. She'd stay up here forever, if she could. It's such a great feeling to be high above the world. Not at all like being high on the balcony of the condo. Here, the wind carries the sweet scent of night. It swirls around her, tickling her on all sides, like it wants to play. Momma doesn't need to know where she is.

Except, she's still screaming, and she's had too much to drink. What if she falls and hurts herself?

Maddie holds tight to the swaying branches and watches Momma circling in the shadows below. She's going to lose her voice if she keeps screeching like that.

It's wrong to stay hidden in the tree. She's got to tell Momma where she is. She lets go with one hand and cups it around her lips and yells down, "I'm up here, Momma. I'm up here in the poplar tree."

Momma hears her, but instead of looking up, she runs out into the grass, screaming, "Maddie? Maddie? Where are you, baby!" She falls into the grass, gets up, runs, and falls again.

Maddie knows she's got to get down fast. Momma needs her.

She takes one last look at the sky. It's so beautiful. The glittering stars. The perfect full moon. Owl's high version of the world is perfect.

As she starts down, she catches a shimmer of lights in the distance. Is it a town, or is it her imagination? She squints, but it's hard to tell if it's real. Maybe it's just the shimmer of stars over the Blue Mountains, or another one of those missing things she needs to be real. If she'd flown away with owl, she'd be there now, discovering what it is.

She can't think about that. She's got to get down and find Momma.

She holds onto the thick trunk of the tree and slides one leg down through the branches. She gets hung-up, and now she can't move. What if she can't get down?

Of course, she can get down. She can jump, if she has to, or she can fly. Maybe Owl will come back and help her do it.

As she struggles to get free, her blue silk pajamas tear and she feels cool air on her knee. Why did that have to happen? Now Momma will think she didn't like playing twins, but she did. She wants to do it again. Tears fill her eyes, and now she can't see. She'll have to let her hands and legs find their own way down. .

Her trapped leg gets loose and her foot finds a strong branch. Good. It's working. Her body knows what to do. She keeps climbing down until she reaches the tight hugging limbs of the lower tree. She pushes free and drops too the ground.

Momma's no longer screaming. Maddie looks for a path of bent over grass, to see which way she went, but even with the full light of the moon, it's hard to find. She yells, "Momma. Where are you?"

The only sound that comes back is that screaming silence. Is she going to lose Daddy and Momma too. Is she going to lose everyone she loves, and be stuck out here in the middle of nowhere by herself with no way to get home?

She runs wildly through the grass yelling, "Momma! Momma! Where are you?"

Nothing but that awful silence.

She doesn't know what to do. She can't leave Momma in the grass all night. What if she fell and hurt herself. She could die. Maddie spins around, trying to decide which way to go, but there's no way to know. She looks up at the sky for Owl and sees the North Star. That could be a sign. Maybe Momma went that way. She heads toward the North Star. Sure enough, she finds Momma sprawled in the grass on her back, sobbing.

Maddie kneels beside her and gently strokes her arms to help her calm down. "Momma, Momma. It's all right. I'm here. I'm right here."

Momma pulls her into a tight hug and rocks her back and forth. "Oh, Maddie. Maddie. I thought you were gone. I thought they took you."

Maddie can hardly breathe, but she whispers, "Nobody took me, Momma. I'm right here."

Momma wails and rocks her harder. "I can't lose another baby. I can't."

Maddie pulls herself free and sits up. "What do you mean, another baby, Momma?"

"My babies. They can't take *all* of my babies."

"I don't understand. Do you mean someone took the baby boy?"

Momma squeezes her arms, and cries out, "Yes, my boy. They took my baby boy."

"Who took him, Momma?"

Momma covers her face and sobs. "I don't know who it was. I turned away for *one* second, and he was gone."

Maddie finally knows who the missing baby is. It's Momma's baby. It means she must have a real brother somewhere. She whispers, "Was the baby my brother, Momma?"

Momma wails, "Yes. Your brother. He's gone!"

"What happened to him, Momma? Please tell me."

Her eyes go wild. "It wasn't my fault. I didn't–."

"Why didn't you tell me I had a brother? I should've known."

She moans. "I didn't want you to hurt like I hurt, Maddie."

"So, that's why you're afraid? Why you won't let me go outside? You're afraid someone will take me?"

Momma nods. "It's not safe in the city, Maddie. We can't go back there. Not ever."

She feels sad for Momma, but she's sad for herself too. She lost a brother without ever knowing him. He must be the baby who cries in her dream house. But he's not just a dream. He's real, and he was probably crying for her to come help. But how could she help if she didn't know he was real? "Where is he, Momma? Where's the baby now?"

"I don't know. He's just gone."

"Is he still alive?"

"I don't know!"

"Is anyone looking for him?"

She bursts into loud sobs.

Maddie tries to comfort her by cooing and brushing back her hair. "We can find the baby, Momma. I'm sure we can, if we try. You and me, and Daddy and Tutor."

"No! I won't go through that again! He's dead. He's gone."

"We can't just give up, Momma. We have to find him."

Momma pushes her back, wipes her face, and struggles to her feet. She stumbles through the grass, mumbling and moaning.

Maddie catches up to hear what else she'll say, but Momma's not talking anymore.

Chapter 22

The sun rises on another worrisome day for Maddie. Momma's been really sick. Ever since she confessed about the missing boy, she's been hiding under the quilt, barely moving for three days. She keeps asking for whiskey, but the whiskey's gone. She won't eat. She won't answer questions. She's so weak from shivering, she can't make it to the bathroom to throw up. It's happened so many times Maddie finally went out back and found an old paint can to put next to the mattress so she could throw up there.

She knows Momma can go without food for a while, but she needs water, or she might die. Every time she tries to give her water, Momma pushes it away, saying, "Whiskey. I need whiskey."

Maddie gets an idea. What if she puts water in the empty whiskey bottle. Momma might think she's getting what she wants? It might work.

She finds the empty bottle, takes it to the bathroom, fills it part way with water, and shakes it. Back in the bedroom, sits next to Momma, brushes her hair back, and gently touches her cheek. "Wake up, Momma. I've got something you want."

Momma moans and pushes her away.

"Please, Momma. Look." She holds up the whiskey bottle and tips it back and forth to show her there's something inside. "Do you want some whiskey?"

Momma grabs the bottle. She takes several gulps, then sniffs the bottle and takes a closer look. "What are you playing at? This isn't whiskey."

"I know, Momma, but I thought you might die if you didn't have some water. I was just trying to help. You're sick. I don't know what to do."

Momma mumbles. "It's okay. It's okay. It's okay." She pulls up the quilt and covers her head. How long will she stay under there this time?

It's going to be lonely again, but at least Momma had some water. She might be okay for a little while, as long as she doesn't throw up.

While Momma sleeps, Maddie lies beside her thinking about her missing brother and where he might be. Momma said he was dead, but that can't be right. He must be in the city somewhere. Or maybe the thief took him to another city? After so much time, it will be hard to find him, but she's got to do it. She can't let him be alone, not knowing he has a sister who already loves him. If she can find him he can come home and be where he should be, and maybe Momma can finally be happy.

But where is he?

There's no way to know.

Momma seems to be sleeping better now. She's not moaning as much or pulling her knees up quite as close to her chest. That's better, but it's still hard to spend the day not doing anything except watching her sleep. Maddie knows she has to find something to do, or she'll go crazy.

She crawls off the mattress, puts on her overalls, and goes to the bathroom to wash her face. She stares into the cracked mirror for a long time, trying to see Mim.

She's not there.

Maddie knows why. Who wants to be in this sad lonely world?

She tiptoes past Momma and out the back door into the light of day. She climbs up on the rock wall, bows to her audience, and steps off her imaginary platform to perform her high wire act. She walks the full length of the wire, holding her bamboo pole for balance, then slips and almost falls, but she's faked it so many times, it's not funny anymore. And now, the high wire is gone, along with the bamboo pole, and the people who were watching. She's back in the stupid boring world of the country.

She jumps off the wall and wanders out into the grass looking for anything alive. A bug, a rabbit, a bird. A bird would be best. She loves birds.

There's nothing but tall green grass. The whole place is boring.

If Tutor was here, they'd talk about how boring it is, and it wouldn't be boring. But he's not here, and who knows if he'll ever be with her again. A sob escapes. "Where are you, Tutor? You're my blood brother. You said you'd watch over me. So why aren't you here?"

She catches a glint of light in the grass and runs to find an old mirror from a car. She holds it up and makes the face of a red-eyed tree frog with Tutor's big grin. The frog melts into the snooty face of the Mad Hatter. It's silly. But so what? She needs some silliness right now.

She tilts the mirror to her eyes. "Really?" she whispers. "Is that you, Mim? How'd you get in there?"

There's no answer from Mim.

"I've missed you so much, Mim. Are you okay? You don't look very happy."

Mim stares straight ahead, with worry in her eyes. Her hair scattered wildly, like it hasn't been combed in years. And why is she wearing those ugly bib overalls?

Maddie slaps her thigh. "Stop it! That's not Mim. Those are your own miserable eyes. Mim isn't real. She never was."

She hurls the mirror across the field and wipes the tears off her face. She's so dumb. Why is she crying? Crying won't help. She needs to think what Tutor would do if he was the one trapped in the country. Would he be like her? Would he hear the silence screaming at him night and day? Would he know how to make it stop?

"Wait." He said she had an *exceptional* mind, so why isn't she using it? Come on. Think. What would Tutor do?

He'd tell her to see things in a different way.

That's right. She needs those conceptual glasses she hid in her suitcase back at the condo. Maybe they will help.

She slips into the bedroom, grabs the sunglasses, and sneaks back out without waking Momma. She sits in the grass with a pair of glasses in each hand. Which pair should she try first: the blue, heart-shaped glasses with sparkling diamond frames, or the pair with dark green frames and pale green glass that bulges out like the eyes of a bug? She'll try those first. If there aren't any bugs in the grass, then she'll be the bug.

But what kind of bug?

When she lays back in the grass and puts the glasses on, she knows what kind of bug she is. She's a praying mantis like the one Daddy gave her when she turned five. Little Sami, with his tiny face. When she talked to him, he'd tilt his head back and forth and look at her in a way that told her he understood everything she said. They'd talk every night before she went to sleep, and every morning when she woke up. Then, one morning, she went to talk to Sami, but he didn't move. He was dead. It broke her heart, but Daddy said she shouldn't be too sad. "It's natural. Praying mantises don't live very long."

Well, it wasn't natural for her to be alone again after Sami died. And it's not natural for her to be alone now, and it's not fair that she lost her little brother without ever knowing him.

She hits her chest with her fist. "Stop thinking like that. Think like a praying mantis. See the world the way a praying mantis does, hanging on a stem all day, trying to be invisible. "

She knows exactly how that feels. She's been invisible since Momma went to bed and stopped talking. Except when Daddy was home, she was invisible at the condo too, until Tutor came.

"Tutor. Where are you?"

It's too sad being a bug. She sets the green glasses aside and puts on the heart-shaped ones. At first, all she can see is that the grass is greener and the sky is bluer. Beyond that, she can't make sense of what the world looks like to a blue heart with rhinestone diamond frames. What could it be?

Suddenly, she knows. It's the lost world of Momma and Daddy's love. They used to have such fun, kidding around making breakfast, playing charades, dancing in each others arms. Did that really happen? Yes, she's sure it did. Maybe it happened before that mean person took her baby brother.

If she closes her eyes, she can see Momma in a pretty blue chiffon dress. Daddy holding her in his arms, as they dance around the living room. After the first song, they gather her in, so she can dance too. That was so fun. Why'd they stop dancing? Were they too sad about losing the baby? Is that when Momma started drinking whiskey?

She remembers something. Something she heard coming from their bedroom at night when she couldn't sleep. She'd press her ear against the wall and hear cooing sounds. Daddy's ooo's and aaah's. Momma's long moans and sighs. Then, Momma told Daddy he couldn't sleep with her anymore. He moved to the other bedroom and the cooing stopped.

Tutor would say all of those things made Momma who she is. All the happy times and the sad times, like when she lost the baby. She understands why Momma's so sad and scared, but what made her not want to sleep with Daddy?

Maddie hears something. A sound, getting louder. There's never any sound out here in the middle of nowhere. She holds her breath and listens. "It's out on the dirt road. Someone's coming."

She runs out front and sees a swirl of dust rising from a pink speck in the distance. It has to be Star's Cadillac. Oh good. She's finally coming back. Now, maybe Momma will get better, and they can do something fun for a change.

Chapter 23

The pink Cadillac slides to a stop in a cloud of dust. Star jumps out in tight white jeans, a shimmering turquoise top, a black silk scarf holding her blond hair back from her high cheekbones, Her shiny pink lips match her car perfectly. She grabs Maddie up and twirls her around, making her legs fly.

Maddie yells, "Put me down, Star. I'm not a baby."

Star twirls her one last time, sets her down, and smooches her cheek with a whimpering look. "No, you're not a baby. But you can still have fun, can't you? You don't have to grow up that fast."

Maddie's about to say, I *do* need to grow up fast, but she sees someone else get out of the car.

Star tips her head in that direction. "Maddie, meet Mouse."

Maddie straightens the straps of her overall, steps forward, and holds out her hand. "Hi, Mouse. It's very nice to meet you."

Mouse looks her in the eye, then dips her head. "Likewise, Maddie."

Maddie can see why she's called Mouse. She's little like a mouse. She has short brown hair, a pointed face, and dark brown eyes that blink and flicker with light. Not only that, she's wearing plain gray clothes. The only thing missing are her whiskers.

Star opens the trunk and hands a bag of groceries to Maddie, another to Mouse. She brings out a bottle of whiskey and says, "Where's your Momma?"

"In bed."

"What? It's practically noon."

"She's been there for three days. She won't talk, or eat, or anything."

Star frowns. "We'll see about that."

They go inside, put the groceries away, and head back to the bedroom. When Star turns on the light, Momma jerks the quilt over her head.

"Oh no, you don't! It's time to get up." Star nudges the quilt down with the toe of her shoe.

Momma squints up at her and mutters, "Is that you, Star?"

"Yes, it's me. Now get up. I've brought Mouse. We've got news."

Momma sees the whiskey bottle and reaches for it. "Give me that, Star. I need it. I've been sick. I've been terribly sick."

Maddie jumps in. "It's true, Star. She's been shivering and throwing up for three days."

When Star hands Momma the whiskey bottle, she takes a long drink, then looks up at Mouse. "Is that really you, Mouse?"

Mouse steps closer. "Yeah, it is. How ya doin'? Not so good, huh?"

"Damn, Mouse. I didn't expect to see you out here in the middle of nowhere."

Mouse blinks and flickers her mouse eyes. "Well…Star tells me you might be needing a lawyer."

Momma shrieks. "What? You're a lawyer?"

Mouse wiggles her whiskers. "Of course, I am. I thought you knew."

Maddie stifles a giggle. Did Mouse really wiggle her whiskers? *Yes,* she did. If Tutor was here, he'd have seen it too. Star and Mouse are fun. And Momma seems to be feeling better. That's good.

Momma struggles to her knees and then up to her feet. She smooths the wrinkles from her blue silk pajamas heads to the bathroom, and turns back. "Uh…why don't you three go out back to the picnic table. I'll get dressed and we can have something to eat or…" She holds up the whiskey bottle and hands it back to Star.

Maddie follows Mouse and Star out back. Star sits next to Mouse on the far side of the picnic table and pours three drinks into plastic cups.

Maddie plants herself on the other side of the table, arms crossed, frowning. "Why'd you have to bring whiskey, Star? It's not good for Momma. It makes her mean."

Star looks at her with sad eyes. "Maddie, your Momma's going through a rough patch right now. It's not easy for her. She needs her whiskey."

Maddie can't believe she's taking Momma's side. "It's not easy for me either, Star, and it's not fair! I want to go back to the city. To Daddy. I need to be home."

"I'm sorry, Maddie." Star looks like she wants to say more, but she doesn't. She gives Mouse a sideways glance, and they both look away.

 Maddie clears her throat and asks the question she's been waiting to ask. "Momma says I have a little brother. Do you know where he is?"

Star looks shocked. "She said that?"

"Yes. But she won't say any more."

Star looks at Mouse. "Well, yes, there was...a baby. I
don't know where he is. He might be–"

"What?"

"Nothing."

Maddie turns to Mouse. "Do you know where he is?"

Mouse shrugs. "No. I don't."

Maddie yells, "Well, somebody must know! He's my
brother! I want to know where he is!"

Star looks past Maddie and shakes her head at Mouse
telling her not to talk. Maddie looks back and sees why.
Momma's by the door showing off her cowgirl clothes. She
takes a pose with one hand on her hip and her head turned
to the side, like she's perfectly fine. It's amazing how
quickly she got better.

Star whistles. "Oo la la. Where'd you get that outfit,
girl? You look like a ro-de-o queen."

Momma laughs and spins around so they can see all
sides of her. She dances over to the table and looks at
Mouse. "Well, what do you think?"

Mouse shrugs and blinks in her mouse way.

Momma smiles and shrugs back, like she doesn't care
if Mouse likes her outfit or not.

It's obvious Mouse doesn't care about clothes, color, or
anything pretty. She's cute like a mouse, but she's plain.
Star is beautiful like the sun, and Momma's beautiful like
the leaves on aspen trees when they turn gold in the fall, or
like the shimmer of a full moon on a starry night.

That's how Maddie remembers her, from another time,
or maybe from her dreams. Momma was beautiful. Now,
with lipstick and her shiny blond hair combed, she's beautiful again, especially in her cowboy girl outfit."

Maddie wants to be beautiful too. She shouldn't have
to wear ugly brown overalls, when Star and Momma are all

dressed up and pretty. She slides off the picnic bench and runs inside.

She only brought two dresses: her pink and purple unicorn dress, and the white satin princess dress she wore when she went flying with White Bird. It has stains, but it's still the prettiest. Momma might not like her wearing a dress, but so what? She can be pretty too, can't she? She'll wear that dress and her new black patent leather shoes. She puts them on.

She goes to the broken mirror in the bathroom and pulls her fingers through her long, ash blond hair, fluffing the curls, as best she can. She steps outside and strikes a pose by the door, like Momma did.

No one notices.

She walks to the table like she's floating on cloud, but they still don't see her. They're too busy laughing and drinking whiskey. Star and Mouse are Momma's friends. Not hers. So what if they're fun? They don't care about her.

She tries to sit at the table, but Momma shoos her away. "Give us some room, Maddie. We've got some serious catching up to do."

Maddie goes to the rock wall where she can sit and at least listen. She can't believe Momma's so selfish. She took her away from Daddy and Tutor, lost the baby boy, was sick for days, and now she won't even let her sit at the table. It's so unfair.

Momma and Star go on and on, laughing and shrieking about things they did in high school and telling jokes about Mouse. Maddie likes the stories, especially the one about skinny-dipping in the Blue Mountain Hot Springs and getting caught. She wants to ask if that's the night Momma and Daddy met, but she knows they won't answer. They don't even know she exists. Right now, she's like her little brother. She's missing.

Momma starts singing a heartbroken cowgirl song. Star joins in with harmony. At the end of the chorus they throw back their heads and laugh uproariously.

Mouse watches the whole thing, sipping her whiskey. She snickers, lips twitching, like she's got a good mouse story to tell, but Momma and Star won't stop long enough for her to tell it.

Mouse glances at Maddie and wiggles her nose. Maddie snickers, but she keeps her own nose still. She doesn't want Mouse to think she's making fun of her, in case it didn't really happen.

Momma slaps the table. "You were the Queen, Star. The dazzling girl on the arm of Jake Quick. What happened to old Jake?"

Star narrows her eyes. "You know damn well what happened to Jake."

Momma laughs. "Oh yeah, he started courting me. Imagine that. Me winning Jake over the notoriously beautiful Star. Course, it didn't take you long to find another Jake."

"You bet I did." Star slaps her leg and hoots. "But tell me something, Jake was a giant. How did you manage?"

Momma gives her a wicked smile. "What do you mean, manage?"

Star licks her upper lip, and takes a soft bite of her lower lip. "Don't play innocent with me, honey. This is Star you're talking to. Remember?"

Mouse shakes her head and looks away like she's fed up with both of them.

Maddie's not sure *what* she thinks of this new side of Momma. She looks beautiful in her cowboy girl clothes.

She's happy and funny and free. That's nice, but why can't *she* be included in the fun?

Mouse bumps Star's arm. "Aren't you going to give her the news? I mean, isn't that why we're here?"

Star slaps her forehead. "Duh. That's right. I almost forgot."

Momma stops smiling. "What news?"

"I'm afraid you two are gonna have to stay out here a bit longer. He's lookin' for you in town, asking everyone if they know where you are."

Momma looks shocked. "He didn't follow you?"

"Of course not."

Momma glances at Maddie, then back at Star, pressing a finger to her lips."

Why doesn't she want Star to talk? Is it because Daddy's in Littletown looking for them? Is that what Mouse meant. If it's true, she has to do something, quick. He might give up and go home. But what can she do?

She has to get back to that power tower she saw when they were driving in. If she climbs to the top, maybe she can see where Littletown is. Then she can go there and find Daddy before he leaves. Momma and her girlfriends don't know she exists. They won't notice she's gone.

She slides off the back side of the rock wall and races around front. Once she's there, she takes a deep breath and looks around. Now that she's alone, she doesn't care about them. She can do anything she wants and be whoever she wants. She's never felt this free before.

She skips down the dirt road in Dorothy's ruby red shoes, singing the song about birds flying over the rainbow. It's the perfect song for a perfect day; the sun straight over-head, a cool wind blowing puffy white animal clouds across the sky. She thinks of Tutor's magic and shakes her sleeves, sending a swarm of honeybees across the field.

She laughs and keeps going, stopping now and then to enjoy her freedom. The grass is dark and tall and green. It ripples in the wind, like there's a wave moving through it. The wave splits the grass, revealing the white bottom of a rabbit just before it disappears into a hole.

That's not a real rabbit. Yes, it is. It's the rabbit from Alice in Wonderland. Alice's rabbit. I'm Alice. It's mine.

She smiles and keeps skipping.

Before long, she sees the power tower up ahead. It looks like a giant man with a pointed head and three arms on each side hanging down at the elbows. Each arm stretches out a wire, linking the Giant to its friends. She'll have to climb past all those wires and arms to see Little-town. If she can see it, she'll go there, find Daddy, and bring him back to get Momma. Then, they can all go home. If Tutor can't go with them, Momma and Daddy can go without her. She's not going anywhere without Tutor.

She kicks through the deep grass toward the tower, imagining what it would be like to live in the real world with Tutor, just the two of them, deciding every day which glasses to wear.

A flock of crows bursts from the grass ahead. They rise, sweeping up to the Giant's top arms, perching there, watching her, cawing loud, like they're calling her to come up and join them.

The crows aren't just birds, they're messengers. Owl must have told Tutor where she is, and Tutor sent the crows to tell her he's coming to save her.

But just in case that's not true, she still needs to climb the tower to find out where Littletown is. That's where she'll find Daddy, if she needs to.

She reaches the base of Giant Man. When she grabs his steel leg, she feels the spark she felt when she first touched knees with Tutor. It's the spark that tells her she's about to learn something new, and it might be scary. She rests her forehead against the Giant's cold steel leg and whispers, 'Tutor, will you help me climb?

The wind carries his answer, "Yes, Maddie. I will."

She sees short bars poking out all along the Giant's leg. They'll make a perfect ladder. It won't be like climbing the poplar tree. There won't be any upward facing branches to hold her on. She'll have to hold herself on. She'd better go slow and careful.

She grabs the first steel rung of her ladder and pulls herself up. That wasn't so hard. She goes up another rung, and another, until she's breathing so hard, she has to stop and rest.

She goes up three more rungs, but she's hardly getting anywhere. Giant Man is really tall. It's going to take forever to get to the top. She calls up to the crows. "Don't leave, crows. I'm coming. I may need your help."

They fly into the air and squawk, saying they'll wait. Their noise brings up more birds, and now the top arms and shoulders of Giant Man are covered with squawking crows. There are so many, and they're so loud, it's hard to focus, but she keeps climbing higher.

She thinks of the story she and Tutor made up about the yellow-haired girl that climbed the wobbly ladder to the secret room in a storm with lightning. What if lightning strikes here? Will it set Giant Man on fire? No, steel giants can't burn. But her hair and her white princess dress might burn.

Too bad. She has to keep going.

The next time she stops to catch her breath, she looks around at the clouds flying in from the Blue Mountains, getting closer and darker. Looks like a storm's coming. There hasn't been any rain in this nowhere place since they came. Why does it have to rain now, just when the crows are about to help her find Daddy?

She looks back in the direction of the gas station. It's been quite awhile since she sneaked away. Do Momma and her friends know she's gone? If they do, are they looking for her? Are they worried?

It's too bad if they are. She needs to find Daddy.

She looks across the endless grass to where she saw the shimmering lights when she was up in the poplar tree. There's nothing there. Maybe it needs to be dark for her to see the lights. Or, maybe she just needs to go higher.

The wind flips her hair into her eyes, and now she can't see. She lets go with one hand, pushing her hair back. Just as she grips the Giant again, a gust of wind rushes through, lifting her skirt, making her feel dizzy and scared.

She's so glad she didn't fall.

Are the crows still there? Yes, they are. They're waiting for her. She better hurry.

Her arms are so tired, and the steel so cold, she can hardly hold on anymore. She rests for a minute, goes up two more rungs, rests again, and goes up two more. When she finally reaches the Giant's lowest arms, she hears a strange humming sound. Is it bees? Are they the bees she shook from her sleeves out on the road? No. Even magic bees can't fly this high. It must be the electricity in the wires that's making her hair rise and her arms tingle

She's not sure what to do.

The hum gets inside her head, growing louder and louder, as clouds fly in, darkening the sky. She has to get to the crows before the storm hits. If it brings lightning, she really *might* catch on fire.

She shouts into the wind, "Be patient, crows. I'm coming. I'm almost there."

More crows rise from the grass, gathering in a huge murder atop the Giant's head and arms. Is there going to be a funeral? Is it her funeral? No, these are Tutor's messenger crows. Nobody has to die.

The crows fly up in a frantic flapping of wings. They circle Giant Man's head, cawing so loud, it hurts her ears. Oh, no. Are they going to leave? "Don't leave, Crows. I need you."

They fly up again, circle around, and settle back down.

Maddie shouts, "Thanks for staying, Crows. I'll hurry."

She tries to climb faster, but the steel stairs take her too close to the buzzing wires.

Don't think about that. She has to get as high as the crows, or she'll never find Daddy. If lightning comes too close, the crows can easily carry her down, or at least help her fly like White Bird did.

She pulls herself up between the Giant's two lowest arms and now she feels electricity from above and below. Her hair's flying in all directions, and there's a strange prickle on the back of her neck.

She's really dizzy. She should go down, now, slow and careful. But how can she do that? She'll fall for sure. She shouldn't have come up this far. Why is it so much harder going down than up?

An icy cold wind hits her face and vibrates out across the wires between Giant Man and his Giant Friends. It whips around her head, flipping her hair and her princess dress around, freezing her bare legs.

She scans the road, wishing with all her lucky stars for someone, anyone, to come along. If they do, will they see her?

Of course, they will. There's nothing else to see out here in the middle of nowhere. And besides, she's the only White Maddie Bird on a Giant Man.

The wind blows in gusts, swirling up dust devils along the road in both directions. As two of the devils get closer, she realizes they're not dust devils. One of them is the swirling dust from a pink car, which must be Star's Cadillac. The other is dust from a long black limousine that looks a lot like Daddy's car.

Chapter 24

Maddie holds her breath as the two cars race towards each other out on the road. Are they going to crash? If they do, they won't be able to help her, and she won't be able to help them, either, if they need it.

At the last second, the cars skid to a stop, kicking up a cloud of dust so high she can't see either one. Were they real? Or did she make it up because she needs someone to help her?

That must be it. No one would be out here in the middle of nowhere, in a storm. No one's coming to save her. Even if Momma and Star realized she was gone, they wouldn't know where to look. If she can't get down by herself, she'll be stuck up here forever. The crows will eat her flesh for lunch, her bones will fall to the ground and get lost in the grass. No one will ever know she was here.

That's not right. The crows won't have her for lunch. The crows are her friends. They're Tutor's messenger birds. She needs to remember that. If she can't get down, they'll bring berries, so she won't starve. The clouds will bring rain, so she won't die of thirst.

As the dust settles, revealing that the cars were real. Isn't that Daddy and Tutor getting out of the limousine?

It's true. Owl really *did* find Tutor. Then Tutor sent the Messenger Crows to tell her he was coming. And now, here he is with Daddy to save her.

She holds on with one hand, leans way out, and screams into the wind at the top of her lungs, "Daddy! Tutor! I'm up here!"

They don't look up, which means they can't hear her.

She waves her loose arm and yells even louder, "Please, Daddy! Look up! I'm on the tower!"

Daddy doesn't hear her and neither does Tutor. It's not that far across the grass to the road, but if it rains harder, and they can't hear or see her, they'll leave. They might go back to the city without her. She has to climb down, fast. Or maybe she better fly down. It would be a lot faster.

She leans back, gripping the steel with only her fingertips, trying to let go. But wait, what if she can't remember how to fly? What if her princess wings won't hold? White Bird's not here to help this time, and the landing will be a lot harder. There's no flowerbed here.

She looks up at the crows. "Please, Crows. Will you help me fly?"

They chatter back and forth, lift up, squawk, and settle back down. They do it again, like they can't decide.

She yells, "Come on, Crows. Make up your minds. We have to fly down now, before they leave."

The Crows make a clicking sound and flap their wings. Does that mean they will or they won't help her fly? Why won't they say?

She looks at the tiny people out on the road. Daddy and Tutor are so small, she could easily pick them up and move them around like a horse or pawn in a chess game. She could move them to the tower and make them look up and see her.

That's not real.

She grips the steel with one hand, swinging back, scanning the world around her. It's scary, but it's wonderful to be up high with the crows, feeling the wind on her face, watching the storm roll in. She's never felt braver. Never freer. She can see herself in so many different ways…simultaneously, like Tutor said. From above, through the eyes of the crows and Giant Man, she's a daring girl who loves high places. From below, she's a White Maddie Bird on a Giant Man.

The driver's side door of the Cadillac opens wide and Momma gets out. Wait! That's not right. Why's Momma driving Star's car?

Momma rushes to the limousine, fists flying, slamming Daddy's chest. He wrestles her arms down, but she breaks loose and hits him again, even harder. Why's she acting so crazy? Is she afraid she's lost a another baby? A girl, this time?

Maddie yells down, "Stop it, Momma. I'm not lost. And I'm not stolen. I'm up here. Leave Daddy alone."

Momma can't hear.

A cold wind blasts Maddie in the face full force. It sends an icy chill up her arms to her neck and she almost lets go. The sky darkens. The crows make that clicking sound again. This time, they sound scared. She's scared, too.

Out on the road, Daddy pats Momma on the back, trying to calm her down. Tutor paces back and forth, scanning the road. Is he searching for his little sister? She wishes she could tell him where she is without Momma and Daddy having to know. If he climbed up, they could see the world through Giant Man's eyes, learning his high, four-direction view. When they've seen enough, they could fly away to someplace fun

No. She can't do that. Momma and Daddy wouldn't know what happened to her. They already hurt too much from losing the baby boy and not knowing where he is. Or even if he's alive. She can't make them hurt even more.

Lightning splits the sky, followed quickly by loud thunder, that rattles the wires, and makes them moan. The crows scatter across the darkened sky with a shattering cry.

Now she's alone, and no one knows where she is. Huge raindrops smack her face and her hair is being pulled out in all directions by the wind.

She looks down and sees Momma and Daddy get in the limousine. Oh, no. "Don't leave, Daddy! Please! Don't leave!"

Tutor runs to the limousine, stops, and looks back. Does he sense she's here?

She yells, "I'm here, Tutor. I'm up on Giant Man."

He doesn't hear.

Lightning strikes again, followed by the instant crash of thunder. Tutor looks up and waves. He sees her. He yells something she can't hear, then he runs to get Daddy from the limousine. Momma comes too.

They run through the grass, wildly waving their arms. Daddy yells, "Stay put, Maddie! Stay right where you are!"

Why are they so scared? She's fine. She climbed all the way up here, didn't she?

When they reach Giant Man, Momma grabs his leg and tries to pull herself up, screaming, "Why, Maddie? Why?"

Daddy pulls her down and holds her in his arms while Tutor scrambles up the Giant like a monkey that's done it a thousand times.

Maddie yells, "Wait, Tutor. The steel's slippery with rain. I better fly down."

"No, Maddie! No! Don't move a muscle! I'm coming!"

"Okay, but please be careful. I can't lose you again."

Another jagged streak of lightning crackles through the dark clouds and sparks along the wires. Thunder comes fast, the rain pounds her head even harder. At least, she won't burn. She's too wet to burn. Her hair is stuck to the side of her face, her princess dress is soaked through, plastered to her legs. The freezing cold steel hurts her hands, and now the buzz of the wires is so loud her ears hurt. No matter what Tutor says, she has to go down, at least below the buzzing wires.

She reaches around with her foot, finds a solid spot, and slides down, being careful not to touch the wires.

Tutor calls out, "No, Maddie! No! Stay where you are!"

She should listen to him, but she can't stand the buzzing, and the whipping wind makes her feel like she's going to be blown across the sky.

Tutor climbs closer, looking up at her with his turquoise blue eyes shining, rain streaking his cheeks like tears. "Oh, Maddie. I should have known you'd be up somewhere high with the birds."

She tries to smile. "Well, the Crows *were* here before. They brought your message."

He gives her a rain-drenched smile. "Oh, yes. My message. I'm glad it got through."

"The Crows said you'd be here any minute, and then there you were. They were a big help, just like Owl. Did Owl tell you where I was?"

"What do you think? Me and Owl are old friends." He looks down, then back up at her. "So, my little drenched Maddie Bird, are you ready to go down?"

She can't believe it. He called her, Maddie Bird, exactly what she called herself. Like always, Tutor knows what she knows.

Now, she's not sure she wants to go down. Not yet. She smiles at him. "You know, we *could* stay up here and listen to the Giant Men talk on their telephone wires. They might have some important things to say."

Tutor tilts his head, listening to the wires. "Hmmm. I believe they're saying we need to get down from here. Quick!"

He squeezes her toe through her drenched patent leather shoe. "So, here's what we're going to do. I'll stay one rung below you all the way down. If you slip, I'll be right here to catch you. Okay?"

"Okay, Tutor. I feel braver now that you're here."

"Brave, you say? Believe me, Maddie, you're the bravest girl in the world."

She loves when Tutor says nice things. She's missed that so much. She's missed him so much.

They start down with him holding the steel on both sides of her, keeping her safe like the upward reaching branches of the poplar tree.

As they go down, one rung at a time, she thinks about the strange days she's had since she met Tutor. Before that, she was just a character in one of her books. Now, she's a real person in the real world, who's learned how to climb tall trees and Giant Man towers. She learned to take care of herself when Momma was so sick. She even took care of Momma.

Her foot misses a rung, and she slips.

She's not falling, Tutor's got her in his strong arms.

She whispers, "I'm sorry, Tutor. I should have been more careful. I was thinking about something else."

"One of your flights of fancy, I expect. Don't worry, Maddie. We're doing just fine."

She feels so safe with Tutor. Her Big Brother, the friend that she's always needed. Now, he's come to rescue her from the country so they can be together again.

He goes down one step, keeping his arms high. "Okay. Here we go. Nice and easy. We might as well enjoy ourselves while we're here. I mean, how many times in your life are you going to find yourself at the top of a high tension power tower in the lightning and rain."

"You mean, on top of a Giant Steel Man in the rain?"

"Exactly."

As they get closer to the ground, she can hear Momma screaming. "Why'd you do it, Maddie? Why? Why? Why?" She's like a broken record that won't stop. If Momma has to know why she did it, it's because she had to find Daddy. But there were other reasons too. She needed to be at the top of the world, where she could see through the all-directions lens.

She needed to know what it 's like to be a real person in the real world. A brave person, who's free to decide things for herself. Yes. That's the answer. She needed to find out if she's smart enough to live in the real world or would she go galloping off the cliff onto the rocks with the bears.

Tutor steps down to the last rung of the Giant's stairs. He moves aside and Daddy lifts her into his arms. He's holding her so close she feels his hot breath on her neck when he whispers, "I'm sorry, honey. I'm sorry. I would have been here sooner, but I didn't know where you were."

"It's okay, Daddy. It's okay. I knew you'd come."

Momma pulls her away from Daddy's arms and hugs her even tighter than he did. She keeps saying, "Why, Maddie? Why?"

"I'm sorry, Momma, but I had to find Daddy. I thought I'd never see him again. I couldn't let that happen."

Momma whimpers and turns her loose.

Daddy lifts Momma's chin and looks deep into her eyes. "Come on, honey. Let's get back to the cars. We're going to drown. We can talk about all this later."

Tutor's eyes are dark and serious, but there's a shine in them telling Maddie she was brave, and that she's learned something important. When they start having lessons again, maybe Tutor will ask her what she learned from Giant Man. Maybe, just this once, she can teach him something he doesn't know.

Chapter 25

Daddy holds his jacket over Momma's head, protecting her from the rain as they head across the grass field. Maddie's so wound up from being up on Giant Man that she can't stand to go slow. She grabs Tutor's hand, and yells, "Come on. I'll race you to the cars."

They race, slipping and sliding through the wet grass. They get to the road at the same time, and lean, hands on their knees, gasping for air and howling with laughter. It feels so good to be happy.

Tutor straightens up and shimmies off the water like a wet dog. He barks twice at the sky, then flashes Maddie a Cheshire Cat grin. "Man, that's a real cats-and-dogs rain."

She meows. "Or maybe it's the torrential tears of a witch crying over spilt milk and the thunder is an old man snoring."

"Oh, you're quick, Maddie. You've definitely got your metaphors and aphorisms down."

"Really?"

"Most indubitably. Not only that, but you paint a very nice picture." He clicks his heels, spinning down the road, kicking up mud as he sings that old song Momma used to sing. "I'm singing' in the rain, just singing' in the rain. What a glorious feeling, I'm happy again . . ."

He comes back, takes her hand, twirls her under his arm, and they dance down the muddy road together, singing, "Singin' in the rain, just singin' in the rain."

Maddie stops to catch her breath. Tears fill her eyes and mix with the rain on her cheeks. She whispers, "Oh, Tutor. I missed you so much. I thought I'd never see you again."

His eyes shine with rain and the mist of his own tears. "I missed you too, Little Sister."

Little Sister. He remembers their blood oath. He really is her brother. He kept watch over her and came to save her, just like he promised.

Momma and Daddy arrive at the cars and the fun flies away. They're drenched clear through, and they don't look happy. Daddy opens the front passenger door of the limousine to help Momma in.

"No. I can't go with you," she yells. "I've got to get that Cadillac back to Star. She's going to kill me."

Daddy wipes the rain off his face and looks around. "Where *is* Star?"

Momma doesn't answer, so Maddie does. "She's with Mouse at an old gas station in the middle of nowhere. Anyway, that's where they were when I left. It's down the road that way." She points.

Daddy frowns, shaking his head at Momma. "They told me that's where I'd find you. Why? Why take her there?"

She shoves him again, harder. "So you couldn't find us!"

Daddy lifts his hands and lets them drop. "Yes, but here I am."

Momma grunts. "Yes, here you are, but I still have to get that car back to Star!" She gives him another push.

Maddie can't believe how mad she is. Daddy's just trying to help.

He takes Momma's hands and tries again. "Honey, please. Get in the car. I can't let you drive in this pouring rain and mud. It's a wonder you made it here in the first place. I mean, you haven't driven, in what, four, maybe five years, and I believe I smell–"

"What?" She yells. "What do you smell?"

"Never mind that." He turns to Tutor. "How about you drive Star's car to that gas station, and we'll follow?"

Tutor salutes. "Sure, Captain. I can do that." He looks at Momma to see if she's okay with that.

She looks uncertain, but then she flaps her hand and says, "It's okay! Go!"

Tutor races to the Cadillac with Maddie right behind. When they're safe inside, he raises an eyebrow. "You sure Momma won't mind you riding with me?"

"She said, 'It's okay so it's okay. And besides, she and Daddy need to be alone so they can work things out."

"Okay then, let's go."

They start down the road in Star's pink Cadillac with Momma and Daddy right behind in the limousine. The windshield wipers lash back and forth, struggling against the downpour.

Tutor glances over. "So, what have you been up to, Little Sister. I mean, besides climbing to high places?"

She lets out a long sigh. "You know. Mostly looking for something to do or listening to Momma moan and groan. After she told me about the missing boy, she crawled under the covers and stayed there for three days without moving, or saying anything."

"Really? She told you about a boy? What boy's that?"

"Remember the baby boy I heard crying in the dream house on the mountain? You know, the house with the orange juice and the galloping bears?"

"Sure. Who could forget that?"

"Well, Momma told me the boy's real. He's my brother."

"A brother, you say. What do you think about that?" He says it like he's not surprised she has a brother, but how can he know that?

"I don't know what to think, Tutor. He's gone. Someone took him when he was a baby, and now no one knows where he is, or even if he's alive. At least, that's what Momma said."

"How'd she come to tell you that?"

"I was up in the poplar tree. She thought I was gone, and she started yelling and running in circles. She ran out into the field, and I thought she was going to hurt herself, so I climbed down. I found her out in the grass, crying. She kept saying, 'Don't take my babies. Don't take them all.'"

I didn't understand what she meant, but then I realized she must mean me and the missing boy. We were both missing, and she thought somebody took us. That's when I asked her if the baby was real, and if he was my brother. She said, 'Yes,' and then she cried even harder. I told her I'd find him, and that you and Daddy would help. She kept crying, and she couldn't stop. When we got back to the gas station, she crawled under the quilt and wouldn't come out. Will you help me find my brother, Tutor? I think that's the only way she'll be happy."

"Of course. I'll help." He goes quiet, and there's a look on his face like he's not sure the baby can be found.

She touches his arm. "I need to find him, Tutor. I really do. He's my brother, and that means he's your brother too."

"That's right."

The Cadillac hits a slick patch of mud and slides sideways across the road. They come to n abrupt stop at the edge of a ditch.

Maddie gasps. "Oh, my gosh. We almost crashed."

Tutor's eyes widen like he's really scared. Then he winks. "No. No. I just thought you needed some fun. You know, a distraction from all the hard things you've been living through." He glances at the rear-view mirror, like he's wondering what Momma and Daddy think of his kind of fun.

As they head back down the road, Maddie stays quiet with her hands in her lap so that Tutor can focus on his driving. She thinks about him sliding the car so she could have some fun, and a sob escapes. "I missed your silliness, Tutor. I missed...so much."

"Now, now, Little Sister. Don't cry. You can't expect to compete with this rain. It's torrential."

She laughs. "I know, but at least it's good for the ducks."

He quacks. "And worms."

She wiggles her fingers in a wormish way. "Mermaids and rivers might like the rain. And oceans, so they can make big waves."

Tutor gets that silly look. He shakes his head, and out come a stream of pink bubbles from his ears.

Are they real bubbles, or are they just something she misses from before? An absent thing?

She wonders what it will be like when they get home to the condo. Will Momma still want Littletown? Or will she be happy to live in the city with her and Daddy? Will Tutor be there? Will Star come to visit? Will Momma finally let her live in the real world?

She points up ahead. "Look, Tutor. That's the gas station in the middle of nowhere. We'll find Mouse and Star there."

Tutor stops the Cadillac in front of the station. Daddy pulls in behind. Star and Mouse are inside with their noses pressed against the steamy glass door, like they're stuck there.

They get out of the cars and run inside, shaking the rain from their hair and clothes, stomping the mud off their feet, making a big mess on the floor.

Star stands to the side with hands on her hips and fierceness in her eyes. She shakes her head at the floor, then turns on Momma. "You haven't changed one bit since high school, have you? Still taking stuff that doesn't belong to you. That's my car."

Momma stares at her feet. "I had to find Maddie. You know that."

"You should've asked."

Momma wipes the rain off her face, meeting Star's scowl. "No. I couldn't. You and Mouse were out in the grass looking. I knew Maddie wasn't there. Something told me she'd gone down the road. Turns out I was right."

Star takes a quick breath. "Okay. But don't you ever pull a stunt like that again." She turns her scowl on Daddy. "So, you found her, huh? I figured someone would let the cat out of the bag."

Daddy scowls right back at her. "What were you thinking, Star?"

Star flips her hand over. "What can I say. She's my friend. She asked for help. I gave it. Are you going to prosecute?"

Daddy gives her a grim look and shakes his head in disgust.

Momma turns to Daddy. "Come on. Let's get my things." She pulls him to the little bedroom in the back.

Maddie goes to get her things, but the door is locked. She puts her ear against the wood and hears a conversation on the other side.

Daddy says, "Please, honey, come home with us. Maddie and I need you."

Momma moans. "I don't know if I can. There are too many bad memories there. I can't get away from what happened. How can you?"

"Look, I'll take some time off work, and we'll figure this out together. We need to face what happened, honey, face it and move on. Please. Stay with me. I love you."

Momma moans and Daddy whispers, "Come here, little darlin'. I want to show you something."

Maddie hears the soft cooing of doves, that she hasn't heard in years. She leaves them alone so they can work things out.

Up front, Star and Mouse are huddled by the counter, whispering, like they're making a plan. Tutor's wandering between the shelves, looking bored. Maddie runs to him. "Come with me, Tutor. I'll show you my poplar tree."

They go outside and run around back. The clouds have blown away, leaving a sparkling blue sky and endless fields of wet green grass.

Maddie points up at the poplar tree. "That's where I was with Owl when Momma thought I was lost and ran out into the field,"

"Wow! That's a tall tree, Maddie. Was it scary coming down? That's always the hardest part, right?"

"It was hard, but it felt safe because the branches were holding me, you know, like you did with your arms on Giant Man."

He smiles and nods. "Yes, I can see how that works."

She races to the rock wall, scrambles up, arms out like a tightrope walker, tipping this way and that, pretending to almost fall. She turns back and gives Tutor a curtsy.

He claps and sparkles his blue eyes. "I see you've learned how to entertain yourself, Maddie. That's good. Course, you already knew how to do that–what with your literary education and your creative mind." He jumps up on the rock wall and does a high-wire act of his own.

"You're a really good tightrope walker, Tutor."

"Why thank you, you're not bad yourself."

They sit down, dangling their legs, clacking their heels against the rock wall. "So, Maddie, what have you learned out here in the country besides your high wire act and climbing skills?"

She thinks about it. "Mostly, I've learned that the country can be just as lonely as the city, if there's no one to talk to. There's hardly any sound out here, except for the wind and the rain, and Owl, and the Crows, once they came. I liked the crows. I like birds a lot, and I like to fly, but I need to be with people too. I need you, Tutor. I want to see the world, you know, through the different glasses, but I want to see it with you. Can we do it together? Please, Tutor."

"I'd like that, Little Sister. You see the world from so many angles even without the glasses. Like I've said before, you learned to live in the heart and minds of the characters you met in your books. A princess or a prince, a pauper or a king. An old man snoring in the rain. You've learned how to see through all those different perspectives. While you were away, I realized something, you should be teaching me, Maddie. Not the other way around."

"That's not true, Tutor. You teach me so many things, you make my head spin." She laughs and waggles her head like it's spinning, knowing he'll remember that's what he said would happen if she listened to him.

It's true. He did make her head spin, and he still does. He'll always be her Tutor, her friend, her blood brother.

They stay on the wall, watching the late afternoon sun glitter rain diamonds in the grass. She hears a whoosh of wings, and a raven flies by. She didn't know there were ravens out here. She loves ravens. They can be tricksters, but they can also bring wisdom and change. Right now, she'll take the wisdom. She doesn't need change, as long as Tutor's with her. She closes her eyes, letting the deep warmth of happiness settle inside her. Please time, stop now. Let me in stay in this moment forever.

She's been needing this feeling for so long. Needing to feel safe and happy. She doesn't know what's going to happen in the future, but right now, everything is perfect.

Chapter 26

The back door of the gas station squeaks open and Daddy calls out, "Tutor. Maddie. Let's go home. We'll meet you out front. I'll bring your suitcase, Maddie."

"Okay, Daddy." Maddie takes one long, last lingering look around and whispers, 'Goodbye, endless grass. Goodbye, poplar tree. Goodbye, little gas station in the middle of nowhere."

They jump off the wall, and she takes Tutor's hand. "Come on. Let's go see what the next world brings."

He smiles. "Yes. Let's do."

They run around front and find Daddy waiting in the limousine and Momma talking to Star. Mouse stands nearby, twitching her nose as she listens.

Star grabs Momma's shoulders and looks deep into her eyes. "You sure about this, honey? You don't have to go back there, you know. You can stay with me."

Momma shakes her head and whimpers. "No, Star. I have to. I told him I'd try." She glances back at Daddy, and whispers, "But can I have a rain check, if I need it?"

Star's face lights up. "Anytime, Darlin'. You're always welcome. And so is Maddie."

Maddie wants to scream, "No, Star. I don't want to be welcome," but she swallows the words and keeps quiet.

Momma and Star share one last hug, and Momma flaps her hand over her head at Mouse as she goes to the limousine. She gets in front with Daddy.

Maddie and Tutor run to the limousine and slide in back. Suddenly, they're in a secret world all their own, a place with a thick sliding glass window that separates them from the front-seat world of Momma and Daddy. Tiny light bulbs encircle the floor, casting up golden light that makes their skin shimmer like figures in a stained-glass window.

Maddie smiles at Tutor. "So, how do you like Daddy's secret stained-glass room?"

He stretches his arms across the top of the black leather seat, like it's a couch in a living room, and glances around with a snooty Mad Hatter look. "Yes. Quite the room. Bigger than most of the places I've lived."

Maddie gasps. "Really? Where do you live, Tutor?"

He shrugs, like he doesn't know.

"Do you live in one of those cardboard houses I saw from the train as we left the city...or on the roof of a tall building where the pigeons sleep at night." She giggles. "I bet you sleep in an actual bird's nest, all curled up with the baby birds. Probably robins."

He gives her a silly grin and flaps his bent elbow wings. "Yes, something like that."

She takes his hand, pressing a kiss to his fingers. 'Please, Tutor, will you show me where you live?"

"Sure. I'd be happy to...if that works out." He glances at Momma in the front seat.

Maddie closes her eyes and imagines herself at Tutor's place. She's in a tiny room with Mad Hatter Tutor serving her peppermint tea and tiny cookies that make her small, or tall, depending on what she needs. The characters from his books jump out and fly around the room, shouting out their lines, getting their stories all mixed up. Tutor's top hat pops off his head and zips around the room, looking for a place to land. It bumps into the walls and sets the story book characters spinning as it flies by. Finally, it comes to rest on Tutor's head where it belongs.

She opens her eyes to Tutor's smile. "Looks like you took a nice jaunt that time, Maddie. Where'd you go?"

She gives him a mischievous smile. "To your place. We had peppermint tea, and I listened to the characters in your books talk. Boy, were they loud."

He gives her a stunned look. "Really? I thought they only talked to me. You must be special."

She smirks. "I *am* special. You know that."

"In fact, I do."

She rests her head against his arm, breathing in deep. "Really, Tutor. When we get back to the city, will you take me to see where you live? I can't go back to living in a condominium cage. I really can't. I need to live the real world."

"I know that, and your Daddy does too. He wants to make that happen."

"I hope he can."

Up ahead, Giant Man rises from the grass. Maddie presses her nose to the window, watching him grow to his full height as they approach, then shrink back down, as they drive away. She whispers, "Goodbye, Giant Man. I'll miss you."

It's true. She *will* miss Giant Man. She'll miss Owl and the Crows. She'll miss the poplar tree. She'll even miss the lightning and the pouring rain. She'll miss Star, and especially Mouse, with her funny mouse ways. She'll for sure miss dancing down the muddy road with Tutor after he helped her down from Giant Man. She'll even miss curling up close to Momma on the floor of the little bedroom.

She's surprised at how many things she's going to miss. She didn't think she'd miss anything about the country, but she already does.

She looks at Tutor. "I don't understand. How can you hate something, then realize you love it just when it's slipping away? I mean, I always loved Giant Man and the Crows. I loved Owl and Star, but before they came, I hated the country. I was sad. I was lonely and bored. I couldn't see how big it was, but now I can." She takes a quick breath. "Do you know what I mean?"

"Yes, in fact, I do, Maddie. Your time out here is important. Moving forward, you'll see how the lessons from the country ripple through your understanding of the past, of the future, of everything that comes your way."

Chapter 27

Daddy guides the limousine around a wide curve, the endless grass fading behind them. They float along a narrow ribbon road through fields of wild violet lupine, golden yarrow, and a pink flower that Maddie doesn't know. A golden stream of light falls across her knees, drawing her gaze upward. "Tutor, was that skylight there before?"

He smiles. "No. I believe Big Daddy just gave us that."

"Oh boy. Pretty soon it will be dark, and we can see stars."

"I'll show you the constellations."

She smirks. "Or, I'll show *you*."

"Right. Should've known. Is there anything Big Daddy *didn't* teach you?"

"He left a few things for you." She smirks again and slides closer, snuggling into the silky smoothness of the black leather and the warmth of Tutor's arm.

Tutor's eyes shine. "So, Maddie, tell me more about your experience in the country and how it's changed your understanding of things."

She lifts her shoulders, and lets them fall. How can she explain what she's only just beginning to understand? "It's too big, Tutor. I don't know where to start."

"Take it slow. We're not going anywhere. Well, we are going somewhere, but it'll take us a while to get there."

She places her hands over her eyes and stares into the darkness, looking for an answer.

"Anything, Maddie. Find a spark and follow it."

"Well, there's one thing that might be important."

"What's that?"

She frowns, still sorting through her thoughts. "It's hard to explain, but it's like what I said before. At the condo, I felt so small. I mean, I was high up, but it wasn't the same as being high on Giant Man. On the balcony, I was like a little bird, stuck in a cage. I didn't think I could do anything right in the real world, that I might gallop off the cliff with the galloping bears."

She stops to think. "Up on Giant Man, I felt as tall and wise as he was. I could see everywhere, in all directions. Back at the condo, I could only see North. If I leaned way out on the balcony, I could glimpse a little East and West, but the tall buildings blocked the view. And I couldn't see South at all. I still don't know what South looks like. I need to go back to the condo, ride the elevator to the roof, and finally see what's been behind me all this time."

Tutor's smile widens. "Maddie, the way you think about all this. Wow!"

"It just keeps coming, Tutor. I think it's because of everything I've learned. You know, from you, and the country, and seeing things in different ways. It's made my mind bigger. Right?"

"It sure has."

"I love it, Tutor. Thanks for teaching me."

"You're welcome, Maddie. But you've taught me just as much. That's how it works. Getting to know someone is like stepping into a new world that's full of surprises, new ideas, and different ways of seeing. If you engage every person you meet with curiosity and an open mind, you'll always learn something new and amazing. With so many people in the world, you'll never run out of lessons."

"I want to learn everything, Tutor. I want to meet all the people and listen to their stories. If they want to hear my stories, maybe I can teach them to think big, like you taught me."

Tutor's eyes turn serious. "Just remember, Maddie, not everyone will want to learn those lessons."

"Why not?"

He sighs. "Because some people don't like the shaky world of endless possibilities. "

Maddie nods. "I understand, but if they get used to it, they might like it, like we do."

"Yes, they just might." He leans back, smiles, and closes his eyes.

Maddie presses her cheek against the cool glass of the window. It's dark outside, dark enough to see the glowing lights of the city up ahead. They're almost home.

The thought of going back to the condo stirs a storm of emotions inside her. She's excited, but she's also scared. What if Momma *won't* let her go to school? And if she does, what if the other kids don't want to be friends? She remembers how Momma and Star left her out of their fun at the gas station. Will the kids at school do that too?

No. That won't happen. If she's curious about who they are, and she listens to their stories, surely, they'll want to listen to her stories too. That way, they can all learn lessons from each other.

One thing she knows for sure, she can't lose Tutor. He opened the world to her when she was locked inside the condo. He taught her things she couldn't even imagine. Now, if they can go out into the world, together, just think how much they can learn.

www.ingramcontent.com/pod-product-compliance
Lightning Source LLC
Chambersburg PA
CBHW070925180626
46817CB00003B/1192